STOLEN LOVE

ELITE MAFIA OF NEW YORK SERIES
BOOK 2

MISSY WALKER

Cover Design: Missy Walker

Editor: Swish Design & Editing

To my loyal readers, I hope this book provides the escape you're seeking x

1

EMILIA

It's not easy shaking off the sense of leaving my life behind as I turn a slow circle in the center of my living room. I want to be sure I take everything I need before we go. After all, I don't know if or when I'll ever return now that I'm moving in with my boyfriend.

That's an understatement. If only life were so simple. My boyfriend happens to be part of a notorious mafia family who, until recently, I was determined to shut down and put behind bars permanently. I'm moving in with Luca because I love him but also to satisfy his father's demand that he be able to watch over me. Until I resigned from my position in the NYPD today, I was the enemy.

In the eyes of at least one family member, I still am.

"You about ready to go?" My partner, or rather my ex-partner as of this morning, steps out of the bathroom and has the nerve to scoff when he sets eyes on my indecisive state. "Come on. It's not like you'll never come back here."

I hate him for being able to see into my head so easily. I hate him for many things. For lying to me and taking money from the Santoro family while making it look like he was doing his job to end their grip on the city. For standing back and saying nothing in my defense when that same family decided whether or not to kill me after I fell in love with the younger son. I didn't mean to do it. I would never have predicted it would be possible. If there's one thing I've learned these past few weeks, it's how impossible it is to predict just about anything in life.

He made me feel small and useless when we were working together, which I now understand was his way of keeping the family safe. Though it's a family I'm now part of, I can't forgive him for lying to me. I don't know that I will ever be able to get past it.

I swallow back the bile rising in my throat at his casual attitude. "You should know they're going to keep a close eye on me. You've been involved with the Santoros longer than I have."

He lifts a shoulder in his usual thoughtless way, studying the trio of small boxes I packed. "This is going to look suspicious. If the neighbors see, they'll want to know why you're leaving. You're supposed to be living here, remember?"

As if I could forget. I can't let anybody know I'm living with Luca or have anything personal to do with him. "Everybody keeps to themselves here except for Mrs. Henderson, who lives next door, and I can always make up something if she sees us."

She's hardly the first thing on my mind when I'm barely an hour beyond my resignation from the force. There I was, a twenty-four-year-old detective, ready to take on the world. If not the world, at least the mob.

Now, I'm moving in with them. I can't wrap my head around it.

He picks up the biggest box full of books and framed photos of my parents and extended family. Even if I don't put them out around the little house I'm sharing with Luca on his family property, at least I'll have them with me. I can always look through them if I'm feeling a little lonely.

It isn't that I'm anything less than thrilled at the idea of starting a life with Luca Santoro. That doesn't make me naïve or blind to reality. There will be times when he's busy with family business, especially with this war looming over us. I'll end up on my own, and I will want every opportunity to comfort myself and remember who I am.

"I guess we'd better get going." It will be easier the sooner we're finished. I've already spent more than enough time with Craig today, going in for a follow-up interview after we first outlined the story that Rocco Santoro put together with Craig's help. A way of explaining why I went missing and why I'm now injured. My right arm is still weak, but it's only been a week since I was shot.

With that in mind, I let Craig take the box to his car and wait for him to return to take the other two. "Cheer up," he urges with a crooked grin as I turn around to take one more look at my apartment before going into the hall and locking the door. "You get to be with your true love now. Isn't that all that matters?"

"Considering you're the one who swears you only take bribes from Rocco to support your family a little better, you're awfully sarcastic about love." His little flinch gives me a surge of satisfaction as I follow him down the stairs.

"You went and fell in love with a killer. That's an entirely different level." He eyes me, smirking, as he stands back to hold the door open so I can step onto the sidewalk and into a bitterly cold morning. "Maybe keep that in mind the next time you want to pull a superior attitude, kid."

This day can't be over quickly enough.

He notices the way my gaze shifts around both before

and after we're in the car. "Relax," he tells me with a snide chuckle as we pull away. "Unlike you, I know how to keep a low profile. There's nobody following us."

Frustration leaves me gritting my teeth. "Do you think they'll want me to come back in for another interview?" I ask. Otherwise, I'd have to tell him exactly what I think of his sarcasm.

"When there's a full-blown war about to explode between the city's most powerful mafia families? Trust me when I tell you the department's resources are better spent elsewhere. You were a kid who got kidnapped and shot before I could get you out of there. You were doing too good a job of tracking the Vitalis and their crimes."

"Detective," I mutter.

"Pardon?"

"You called me kid. *Again*. I was a detective before I resigned." I blink hard, forcing back the tears threatening to well in my eyes.

I worked so hard.

I was so proud.

Now I have Luca, and the thought of him alone is enough to soothe me. It's like a warm blanket draped around my shoulders, wrapping me in a sense of comfort. He loves me. If it hadn't been for him, I would've been run over and killed. I would have been murdered either by the Vitalis or his own family, all because I came too close. Granted, that was the result of my eagerness and determination to make my mark. I don't think I can be blamed for it, but I can admit now that I might have been foolish to think I could single-handedly take down a powerful family with connections all over the city and beyond.

What difference did I believe I could make?

Getting home to Luca is the only thought that keeps me

in one piece as Craig drives us from Brooklyn to the Santoro family compound on Long Island. He might be certain we're not being tailed, but that doesn't mean he can't be careful, taking a longer route.

It isn't long before I identify the gray stone walls ahead, like the barrier around a castle.

Does this make me a princess?

In the grand scheme of things, I could do much worse than living on the grounds of a sprawling estate. The house Rocco built for Luca is more than comfortable—charming even. Ironically, I'm sure it's much safer than the apartment I called home until recently. The real threat is everything taking place outside the thick walls built around the property's perimeter.

Maybe not entirely. Craig pauses momentarily at the iron front gates, where an armed guard standing sentry gestures for the guard in the gatehouse to let us in.

A sleek black car is on its way out. It's inhabitant rolls down the rear driver's side window so he can menacingly glare as we cross paths.

Dante.

He didn't need to roll it down since the tinted window still allowed him to stare at me. He did it so I would know he was staring and remember how deeply he resents my presence on his family's property. The icy hatred in his eyes makes my stomach churn.

Craig emits a soft whistle, then shakes his head, chuckling darkly. "I wouldn't want to be in your shoes, kid," he mutters as we continue down the wide gravel driveway.

If there's one thing I'm experienced with, it's ignoring his stupid comments and pretending they don't bother me. I have to rely on that experience as I stare out the window, trying my hardest not to tremble. Dante wants me dead. He doesn't care that his brother loves me or that I've turned my back on everything I once thought mattered for his sake. He's bitter that his father took my side, at least as far as Dante's concerned. I know Luca will keep me safe, but that doesn't make it any easier to endure Dante's resentment.

Craig stops in the wide, circular courtyard in front of the dramatic staircase leading up to the mansion's entry. A pair of guards are stationed there, staring down at me as I step out of the car.

Craig calls up to them, "Can somebody around here give me some help getting these boxes over to Luca's?" One of the black-clad men jogs down the stairs while I continue to stare at the sprawling house.

My nerves tell me somebody is watching me. I'm sure of it. But I belong here. Luca wants me here. With this in mind, I can roll my shoulders back and lift my chin, ready to face whatever's coming next.

One of the tall double doors swings open as I watch. Suddenly, the day is not so cold or gloomy. The sight of Luca rushing down the stairs is a ray of warm, dazzling sunshine, lighting up even the darkest corners of my heart. A soft sigh of relief escapes my parted lips before he reaches me and lifts me off the ground in a fierce hug.

"How did it go?" he asks, setting me on my feet without letting go. His dark eyes search my face with an almost hungry look. I don't know whether he's hungry for information or me. Probably both, and my body warms at the thought.

"Fine, I think," I whisper with a soft laugh. I'm too happy to be with him to care much about anything else.

"And you have your things?" His brows draw together, and a growl stirs in his chest. "You look upset. That prick Craig didn't give you any shit, did he?"

He did, but I'm not trying to get him killed. I might hate him, but he's still a husband and father. "It doesn't matter. I have what I need." And it's right here, holding me, reminding me why it was so easy to fall in love. I forgot everything I wanted and dreamed about without thinking twice. There simply wasn't a choice to be made. One minute, I hated him. The next, I couldn't live without him.

I place a hand against his chest, feeling the strong beat of his heart. "Will you do something for me?" I ask.

He doesn't keep me waiting. "For you? I'd burn down the fucking world." His eyes darken as his breath fans my face, and I believe him.

My heart swells with love, and I whisper, "Take me home."

2

LUCA

Emilia is everything that was missing from my life.

Lying here, holding her against me, listening to her soft breathing while she sleeps soundly in my arms is a gift. I'm overwhelmed, so full of emotion, I don't know what to do with it. It tightens my chest and closes my throat until it's barely a pinhole, but I realize I wouldn't change a thing.

This perfect creature. She loves and trusts me. I'm humbled that she would consider me worthy of her.

We're expected up at the house for dinner in less than an hour. I should wake her and shower, but that would mean ending this moment. My heart sinks at the idea, and the sensation holds me in place under the thick, down comforter.

"We have to get up soon, don't we?" It's barely a mumble, but the regret in her voice is evident.

"We don't have to," I remind her in a whisper, stroking her hair now that I know she's awake and I'm not afraid of disturbing her rest.

"Sure, we do." She lifts her head, leaving her dark hair to

trail across my bare chest. "We have to behave ourselves. Your dad voted to keep me alive, but there are conditions." She's trying to be brave for my sake, but the slight tremor in her voice breaks my heart a little.

The truth in what she says hurts. She's right. There are conditions he's going to expect us both to abide by if there's any hope of keeping her here with me. "Wait and see." I put on a playful grin for her sake. "He'll love you just as much as I do before long."

She only snorts and rolls her eyes. "I know you're trying to make me feel better, but you don't need to lay it on that thick." There's love in her voice, though, and a smile tugs the corners of her full lips.

"I mean it. He'll come around. Besides..." I wrap a strand of her hair around my finger, admiring its softness. She is unbelievably soft from head to toe, something I could become addicted to. If I'm honest, I already have. "He's nothing if not a sucker for my mother's opinion. Guilia too. And they both adore you."

"I guess that's something the Santoro women have that the men sorely lack." She arches an eyebrow, smirking. "Good sense."

All I can do is sigh in resignation. "You won't get an argument out of me on that."

When I roll over, I lower my body over hers, between her parted thighs. I could die here, wrapped in her, with nothing and no one between us. I plan on pleasuring her in every way imaginable for as long as possible for the rest of our lives.

Reaching between us, I guide the head of my cock to her tight entrance. I close my eyes, giving myself over to the sensation of sinking into her wet heat. Inch by inch, I claim her, or is she claiming me, drawing me deeper, pulling me in with her legs around my hips?

She wraps her arms around my shoulders, holding me close against her firm, supple body. "We need to get going," she breathes out, moaning and closing her eyes. Then she arches her back to meet my slow, deep strokes.

Like I care. "We will go when I've finished with you," I remind her before driving my cock in deeper.

She throws her head back in sheer ecstasy, and a low growl reverberates in my throat at the vision laid out for me.

"Yes, fuck... more, Luca," she moans out, and my name is a plea on her lips.

"You'll take everything I give you like a good girl," I remind her, but who am I kidding? She will never have to beg.

I slam into her harder and faster as I devour her lips, my tongue sliding with hers. Her nails dig into my back, and her pussy spasms around my cock, moaning out her release. A shudder racks my body as her walls clench around me, and my balls draw up. I drive into her a few more times, grinding into her as I come. The aftershocks of my release have me rocking into her, needing to be as deep as possible, her pussy milking every last drop.

Catching my breath, I pull back and tip her chin so our eyes draw level, "Such a good girl."

Her delicious lips turn up, a smile spreading as her hands snake around the nape of my neck. "Mm-hmm."

I'd be tempted to take her again if it weren't for my family.

A HIGH-PITCHED FEMALE voice rings out loud and clear. "You're here!"

I can't help but smile at my beaming sister practically skipping toward us as we reach the dining room with a few minutes to spare. Emilia's hand is tucked tightly into mine. It's going to be quite a while before she feels comfortable walking these halls, and I'm not about to rush her. Only I can make her feel safe.

Guilia's warm reception eases some pressure on my fingers as Emilia loosens up. "Hey, you. You look so pretty in that sweater," she tells Guilia, reaching out to run a hand over her arm. The pale blue cashmere does look nice on her, though. I have to admit I never pay much attention to things like that.

"You can borrow it anytime you want." As always, my sister's generosity and pure heart stir my affection and admiration. There have been times I've wished I could be as naturally warm and kind as she is. She is the sunshine in all of our lives, and for years, she and our mother have been the planets we merely revolve around like satellites.

"Actually, I have a better idea." Guilia's smile widens when she looks over my shoulder.

I hear Papa's familiar, heavy footfalls and look behind me to find him entering the dining room. "Good evening," he says in his usual gruff manner. Right away, I hear the fatigue in his voice. He usually goes out of his way to conceal it in front of the women, but we aren't normally standing at the threshold of war.

Now that Alessandro Vitali has made a move on behalf of his ailing father and destroyed two of our most critical container ports as a means of revenge for not handing Emilia over, there's no point in pretending we aren't about to engage in something bloody.

Guilia isn't interested in any of that as she hurries across the room, wearing a big smile. "Papa, I want to take Emilia shopping. Now that she's living here, she needs new clothes and other things." She kisses him on one sagging cheek before draping an arm around his waist and letting her head rest on his shoulder. "We can go, right? We'll be careful."

"There you go again," Dante grumbles as he enters the room, barely glancing up from his phone long enough to scowl at our charming little sister. "Bombarding him as soon as he's in the room."

I understand something Dante never will. Papa needs the balance Guilia brings to his life. Like now, for instance, when he cracks the first genuine smile I've seen all day. "We'll see."

Guilia turns to us and winks before grinning. She knows that means yes. Emilia laughs softly while I remind myself that it's perfectly fine for the love of my life to go off and do her own thing now and then. She needs room to breathe. I loathe the idea of letting her out of my sight, but I can't hold onto her too tightly. Loving her means giving her a little freedom within limits.

"You'll be guarded the whole time," I assure her in case she's worried. "You'll be safe."

She looks up at me with a knowing grin, then whispers, "Are you trying to convince me or yourself?" She sees through me, a concept that should be terrifying but leaves me wanting to sink into her more. More of my trust and faith—I see it all reflected back at me in her loving gaze, which makes it all worthwhile. I know what an incredible thing I've found, and I'm not about to let anything get in the way. Not even myself.

Mama's already pleasant expression turns into a wide, brilliant smile when she enters the room and sets sight on the two of us. "Francesca informs me that dinner will be coming out shortly," she announces, waving Emilia over to her. It's been a few years since a slip and fall ended in my mother breaking her knee, and Papa insisted on bringing in our chef, Francesca, to keep her off her feet. She's gotten used to it over time but insists on supervising.

"Come, sit with me. You don't know how wonderful it is to have another woman in the house. I can't seem to interest my oldest child in finding a nice girl."

Dante sounds like he's choking, shifting uncomfortably in his chair. "I've been a little too busy for that," he points out in his usually stuffy way. Like he's above a relationship, but I can't pretend I haven't felt the same way.

Before Emilia, settling down was the last thing on my mind.

Mama rolls her eyes at her oldest son. "Honey, it takes no time at all to make a girl want to stick around if you know what you're doing."

Emilia bursts out laughing, quickly clapping a hand over her mouth, and the sound leaves me laughing with her. The pleasure of watching Dante flush with embarrassment is icing on the cake.

The only person who doesn't seem to be enjoying this is the man already seated at the head of the table. Staring across its length, his gaze is unfocused as if he sees something far away. Something none of us can see but him. He's understandably distracted by everything he's juggling now.

Emilia sits at Mama's right, and I sit beside her, keeping an eye on my father. There's something off with him. A glance at Dante reveals nothing since, as usual, he's got his head so far up his ass he barely notices anything around him.

Once Francesco and Niccolo join us, it's time to start the

meal. We know better than to discuss business at the dinner table, but the meaningful glances exchanged between my cousins and me tell a story of their own. We're in a holding pattern, playing it cool, refusing to take the bait Vitali has dangled so enticingly in front of us. Meanwhile, Papa and Dante are hard at work gathering our allies, ensuring we tighten the ranks and strengthen any weak spots.

"How are you?" Mama asks Emilia in a warm, caring tone.

"I'm fine, thanks," Emilia assures her. I can almost feel the gratitude rolling off her. Considering the icy reception from the men at the other end of the table, it must feel like a miracle to be accepted.

"Everything went well today?" Mama prompts in a softer voice, barely shy of a whisper. Emilia's head bobs up and down. I wish I knew whether she's merely reluctant to speak about her resignation openly or if there's emotion behind her silence. Pushing her to open up won't do any good, but I have to try in time.

I look to the other end of the table. Papa is in a world of his own, unmoving, almost unblinking until I clear my throat. It's a relief when he jumps a little. At least he's alive and breathing. "I'm tired," he confesses when I continue staring at him in concern.

"Can't imagine why," Dante mutters while typing on his phone. The screen's glow casts a sickly light over his face, not that he didn't already look like shit. As underboss, he's feeling the strain.

Momma clears her throat, a not-so-subtle cue to put the phone down at the family dinner.

"Why don't you shut the fuck up?" I grit out through clenched teeth. Emilia is deep in conversation with the other women, so she isn't privy to that comment.

"Boys, stop fighting." My cousin, Niccolo, winks at Papa, trying to lift everybody's spirits the way he always has. "You're both pretty."

Papa snorts. It's better than sitting there with a blank face, I guess. "They won't be so pretty after I knock their heads together for bickering like toddlers. The time is going to come when we all need them to step up."

"Not for years yet," I insist flatly. It's a reflex. I'm not about to entertain the idea of him stepping down anytime soon. I don't want to consider the implications for him, the family, and the business.

He barely manages the ghost of a smile, sitting up straighter and reaching for the platter of meatballs and sausage. "So, Guilia," he calls out with a fatherly sigh. "You'd better not plan on making too big a dent in my platinum card with this shopping trip."

We put on a front for the women and kids, sheltering them from the worst of what our world involves. It's what we do. I never understood until now how painfully obvious the act is and how the women only pretend to buy it.

The way I'm pretending to buy it now.

3

EMILIA

The knocking wakes Luca before it wakes me. I roll over when he gets out of bed, barely conscious of anything other than his weight shifting the mattress. Slumber overtakes me again until there's another knock at the front door, and now I understand I didn't dream the first one.

Luca pulls on his pajama pants, which ended up on the floor last night after I stripped them off him. He gestures for me to stay in place, then leaves the bedroom while I push myself up on my elbow and try to wake up in case something important is happening.

The front door opens a moment later, followed by Luca's exasperated groan. "What the hell are you doing here this early?" he asks, and the obvious irritation in his voice tells me it's not his dad or brother or even one of his cousins.

"I wanted to know if Emilia wants to go shopping today."

Sleep is nothing but a memory when I identify Guilia's chipper voice. I fumble around on the nightstand, trying to find my phone in a room where blackout curtains leave me with no sense of day or night. *It's already past nine o'clock?* I guess that's what happens when you spend most of the night fooling around the way we did.

"It's not even that early," Guilia points out, and I press my face to the pillow to muffle a laugh. She isn't wrong, but things like responsible bedtimes tend to get overlooked when you're still in the honeymoon period.

"You could have called or texted," Luca points out. "Just because you have a new friend here doesn't mean I need you coming over unannounced."

"Um... hi. Since when do I need to call before I come over? Stop acting like I'm a stranger, for God's sake." It seems like nothing bothers her. Maybe that has to do with all of the strong male energy she's been raised around. You can't grow up weak or afraid to speak up for yourself in an atmosphere like this. You need to fight to be heard. That much we have in common, even if the reason behind it is slightly different.

Luca's broad shoulders fill the doorway once he reappears, looking down at me with a regretful smirk. "I guess you heard that," he murmurs.

How could I not? "You mean the conversation that took place twenty feet away? Yes, I heard it," I whisper, but apparently. I'm not quiet enough.

"I'm sorry!" Guilia calls out from the living room. "I can make coffee or something while you get ready."

Luca turns around to face her, blocking her view so I can quickly grab his discarded T-shirt lying at the foot of the bed. She does not miss a trick. All it takes is one look at what has to be my epic sex hair and her brother's almost constipated expression for her to slap a palm to her forehead. "Geez. I'm sorry. I wasn't thinking. You guys are probably, like, pawing at each other all the time."

"Jesus Christ," Luca groans out, closing his eyes. "I am

not in the mood for this conversation now or ever. I'm going to get in the shower and pretend this never happened."

"I'll go back to the house," Guilia whispers, wide-eyed. "Really, I'm sorry if I interrupted anything."

"You didn't," I reply with a grin. "Give me, like, twenty minutes. I'll shower quickly and meet you up at the house."

"But Luca just said he was—" Her olive complexion goes dark red before she waves her hands around and shakes her head. "Nope. Not going to think about that. I'm going to leave and crawl into a hole where I never have to imagine my brother showering with anybody." She's still muttering to herself as she leaves, and I somehow manage to wait until she's gone, then burst out laughing.

I've never had siblings, so watching the dynamic play out between Luca and his sister is sort of cute too. And it's shockingly easy for her to make the hardened criminal blush.

Somehow, we manage to keep our shower quick and to the point rather than getting sidetracked. Considering I'm still a little sore from last night, that's probably for the best. It feels like there's never enough time to get to know each other, to explore each other's bodies, what makes us feel good, and how we best fit together.

We're getting dressed when Luca grumbles, "I hope like hell she didn't give everybody a report when she went back up to the house."

The thought of Rocco Santoro knowing what we do in our alone time sets my teeth on edge. I fight back my disgust for Luca's sake, maintaining a playful grin as I pull on a pair of jeans like the ones Guilia was wearing. "We're all adults, right?" I tease, though I don't feel nearly as lighthearted as I pretend.

He turns his back, shaking his head as he looks through his closet. "This is different."

My heart sinks when I hear the flat tone of his voice. "Because of who I am?" I whisper. "Or was, since I resigned?"

Right away, he forgets the black sweater he was about to wear in favor of taking me by the shoulders and looking me in the eye. "That is not what I meant. I need you to know I'm never going to let their feelings about who you are and what you used to do change anything about us. Do you understand?"

I'm almost too overwhelmed by his intensity to speak. I settle for nodding, wide-eyed.

"You're not in any danger," he adds with a frown, his fingers pressing against my shoulders tighter than ever. "You're safe. You're mine, which means you fall under the family's protection."

My heart swells with love, but a healthy dose of confusion is mixed in. "Then I don't understand. What's the problem? It's awkward, sure, but—"

He releases a sigh, cutting me off. "You're the first."

I know that can't mean what it sounds like. "First, what?" I ask, needing clarification.

His jaw clenches like he's in pain as he forces it out. "The first relationship."

I blurt out the first word that comes to mind. "Seriously?"

He narrows his eyes. "You have a problem with that?" he asks with a growl.

"Of course not. I just figured you would've found somebody before me." I run my hands over his bare chest, then take his face between my palms. "Look at you. You're gorgeous. You mean there weren't women cutting each other's throats to get close to you?"

"That should tell you how special you are." He touches his lips to the tip of my nose, then pulls back, sighing. "Now that I've spilled my guts this morning after facing my kid sister's invasion, this topic is officially closed. You're won't get me to sit around and share my thoughts. This isn't a therapy session."

His first relationship. It's not like I've had dozens of them myself, but I've had boyfriends in the past. I understand the need to guard himself and his family against random outsiders, but it strikes me as a little sad he's never felt like he can open up to anybody.

"Now try to have fun today," he urges a few minutes later, as we're about to part ways upon entering the main house. He's heading toward his father's study while I wait for Guilia downstairs in the hall.

"We're going shopping. How could I not have fun?"

He already knows me too well, giving me a shake of his head while he purses his lips like he disapproves. "Try not looking like you're on your way to the guillotine," he murmurs. "It might be easier to believe you."

Guilia finds us before I can protest. "We can stop off for Starbies on the way or something," she assures me, wrapping her arm around mine and then giving her brother a thumbs-up. "No worries. I'll take good care of her." He doesn't look convinced, going so far as to have a brief, muttered conversation with the pair of guards waiting for us at the front door. I didn't realize they were coming with us, which is naïve on my part. I need to get used to having men watching my every move sooner rather than later.

Guilia is blissfully unaware of my conflicted thoughts as she leads me to the waiting car. "This is going to be so fun."

She's right. It will be fun, just as long as I can dislodge the stick from my ass and enjoy myself.

"OH MY GOD. YOU NEED THIS." Guilia's enthusiastic declaration steals my attention from a gorgeous display of designer handbags. We've been in Saks for half an hour, and Guilia has already grabbed at least a dozen pieces she wants to try on while I've followed behind her along with a sales-person who looks like she's glad she works on commission today, even if she appears intimidated by the hulking guards shadowing us.

One look at the price tag on the sleeveless black de la Renta dress she chose knocks the wind out of my lungs. "I couldn't possibly," I tell her with a breathless laugh.

She blinks her big, brown eyes, looking from me to the dress like the dress is the problem. "Why not?"

Why not? I look back and forth before lowering my voice to a whisper. "It's so much money!"

Another blink. "Yeah?"

The thing is, she isn't playing the part of the carefree, spoiled princess. This isn't a joke. She simply doesn't see what the big deal is because she was raised in this world. It's all she's ever known.

She must finally see the confusion and concern on my face for what it is because she turns to me with a serious expression. "You want to be part of our family? Tell me the truth. Do you?"

What is that tightness in my chest? Where does my hesi-tation come from? Because I open my mouth, prepared to rattle off the obvious answer, but nothing comes out. I can't form the words intended to assure her. I settle with an honest reply. "I want to be with Luca. I want to be a part of his life. I want to be part of his world. And if that means also being part of your family, then that's what I want because I want him, and I want him to be happy."

She's a shrewd kid. Her eyes narrow slightly, and her nostrils flare before her lips twitch. I realize too late she's trying not to laugh. She loses the fight, and a giggle bubbles up. "Sorry. I shouldn't have put you on the spot like that. It's something Dante is always getting on my case about." She rolls her eyes, telling me exactly what she thinks.

"It seems like he gets on your case a lot," I observe as gently as I can. "I'm an only child, so I wouldn't know how that feels."

"It's not fun. But we're not talking about me," she points out, and any lingering feelings she has over her brother dissolve. "We're talking about you. And I might be the youngest of the family, but I know what's going on."

"You don't have to tell me that," I remind her with a grin. "Remember? You were sort of my lifeline when I was locked in that room, recovering."

"I know it's not easy for you." She bites her full bottom lip. Does she know how much she looks like Luca? Especially when she's worried, they both get the same little lines between their eyebrows. "And once you get past how weird everything is, you'll want to fit in. Is that not true?"

"It's true," I admit. "I want to fit in."

"That means you need to start getting used to spending some money on yourself." When I open my mouth to protest, she practically sticks a hand in my face, draping the dress over my shoulder. "Listen to me. I know what I'm talking about. You're a nice person, and Luca wants you to be happy. So don't beat yourself up for spending a little money."

"It's not my money," I remind her in a whisper, taking the dress. The quality is obvious from the first touch, but it's over three thousand dollars. I can't make it seem like a logical purchase.

"What difference does that make?" she asks with a soft laugh. "If Luca bought it for you, the money would be coming from the same place."

And that's it. That is the fact that sits at the heart of my hesitation. She doesn't know it, but she cut to it without trying. I know where that money came from. I know how many lives have been affected by the Santoro family's business. Drugs, mostly, but they also ship weapons and run illegal gambling establishments. Sports betting, card games. How many tuition payments have gone into their pockets? Whose house went into foreclosure so I can afford to buy a de la Renta?

I want to be with Luca more than anything. I want him to be happy with me and proud to have me on his arm. One day, we might have a house full of our own family the way his parents do. The idea brings an image to life, one of love and laughter, and warms my heart.

If only I could make myself forget what I know to be true.

"Come on," Guilia urges, already moving along. "We'll try these things on and then have lunch at L'Avenue. It's a little pretentious, but the food's amazing. After that, we can look at shoes."

"I'm in your hands," I murmur, dazed, conflicted, and trying like hell to keep the idea of blood money out of my head.

4

LUCA

"I'm not sure I should let you out in public, looking like you do." My hand closes over Emilia's knee as we ride in the back seat of my BMW. Vinny is behind the wheel, and I smile to myself when I remember how furious I was at his fuck-up when he didn't lock my office door and allowed Emilia to stumble in. While I haven't exactly gotten over my irritation at his mistake since it reflects on what a dumbass he can be, on the flip side of the coin is the fact that Emilia sits beside me now.

Beneath a long coat, she wears a black dress that looks like it was made for her, one that hugs her curves and sets off her perfect tits and ass. My mouth waters at the sight of her lush beauty, and my hand begins creeping up her thigh before I can help it. Not that I could if I tried.

"Your sister insisted I buy it," she tells me, looking down at herself like she's still unsure.

"My sister has good taste." Finding Saks bags in the bedroom after their shopping trip earlier this week was a relief. I was half-convinced that she would refuse to buy anything out of guilt or fear of repercussions. No doubt my sister bullied her into it, though Emilia didn't share too much about the trip when I asked her. Guilia knows how to get her way.

"So you approve?" she asks, sounding full of doubt.

Rather than provide a verbal response, I take her hand and place it over my erection. A smile stirs her lips, and her fingers move ever so slightly, teasing a groan out of me. "What do you think?" I ask with a growl that makes her giggle. At the same time, every possessive instinct I have rears up at the idea of other men seeing her looking like sin on two legs. That's the peril of being in love with a beautiful woman.

Especially when you're a man like me who would gladly cut the hands off anyone who dared lay a finger on her.

It was either bring her with me during my first night back at the club or leave her at home. I can't stand the idea of spending time without her, and we could use an evening together that doesn't involve a family dinner or hanging out around my house.

It's clear she likes getting dressed up. She's been smiling ever since we left, and her excited energy fills the car along with the sweet, floral perfume she wears. It's a combination that leaves my head spinning in the best way.

In the couple of weeks since she was shot, her arm has healed at least cosmetically. There's little more than a couple of scars to mark where the bullet entered and exited. Her leg is much better, too, with barely more than a faint shadow of a bruise left to mar her otherwise creamy thigh.

This is her first night out since everything went down. I want it to be good for her. On the other hand, I also have work to do. Niccolo has stepped up to keep an eye on things in my absence, but there's a reason he isn't more active on the business side of things. He's not a numbers man. He's a killer, plain and simple.

Even with the prospect of a mountain of shit to work through, I can't pretend there isn't something exciting about arriving at the club, stepping into the familiar atmosphere once we've parked, and I've ushered Emilia past the crowd on the sidewalk that parts as if by magic. There's a pulse in the air, like a heartbeat, and I didn't know until now how much I thrive on it.

At the last second, she looks up at me, eyes wide. "You're sure this is safe?" she whispers. "There's nobody here who might recognize me from my old job?"

"Don't worry about it," I assure her. "Craig has it worked out. I made sure first. Any reports on club activity go through him before they reach his superiors, and for the most part, it's cops on the payroll who patrol the area. We're safe." I want to give her a reassuring smile, but she still looks troubled. It's probably because she's still learning how much corruption went on around her.

All eyes turn our way as revelers notice us cutting through the crowd with Vinny leading the way. The bartender snaps to attention and begins working faster. The bouncers stand a little straighter, too, and the girls running bottle service smile brighter when they notice me. There's something to be said for the boss showing up. All the while, Emilia walks beside me, my arm around her waist to keep her close.

Entering the office, Nico sits back in my chair and heaves a sigh. "Thank fuck," he groans out, scrubbing both hands over his face. "I am not cut out for this shit."

"If I find out you fucked up, you're dead." I give my cousin a narrow-eyed stare, then smirk like he does as we trade places behind the desk. We know each other too well. "The building is still standing, and everybody's spending money out there." Still, he winces. "I'm going to remind you of this moment once you take a closer look at things and decide you want to kill me." Niccolo looks toward a grinning Emilia. "I have you as a witness, don't I?"

"No worries," she assures him, her grin widening. If she's put off by being here, she doesn't show it. There's no shadow over her face, no uncertainty, and no memories of what she saw the night we met.

"Are you going to stick around?" I ask as he moves toward the door. I imagined we'd spend time with him catching me up on what I've missed, but he's acting like he set a fire in one of my drawers and wants to leave before it engulfs the room.

"I would," he tells me, his hand grasping the door knob. "But to be honest with you, if I never hear dance music again as long as I live, it will be too soon. I've never craved peace and quiet like I do now."

I can't blame him. The walls are soundproofed well enough, but there's still a constant pulse reverberating in the walls and floor, thanks to the volume of the music blasting out there. "Fair enough. Get the hell out of here." Just as he's leaving, I add, "Thanks. Really. You're a lifesaver."

"Again, I'm going to remind you of that."

He leaves, and Emilia giggles. "I like him. Is that weird?" she asks.

"Depends on what you mean by the word 'like,' " I point out with a growl.

Her smile turns to a knowing smirk as she rolls her eyes. "Give me a break. You know what I meant."

"If anything..." I point out while pulling her into my lap,

"... that should tell you something. None of us are monsters out of a horror movie."

"That's true." Yet something washes over her lovely face. Uncertainty? Conflict? Whatever it is, I hate seeing it.

"Come on," I decide, easing her off me only moments after pulling her close. "Let's get out of here and have a little fun. You deserve it."

"You have work to do, don't you?"

"That can wait. Besides, more than half of this job is showing my face, bullshitting with customers, and I haven't done that in too long. And maybe..." I continue while running a hand over her ass on our way to the door, "... I want to show you off a little bit just so everybody knows you're mine." My fingers press against her flesh, and her eyes darken in understanding. One thing I never have to worry about is whether or not we're on the same page physically. We're a pair of magnets drawn to each other.

Emerging from the hall, I signal for the server closest to us, then survey the dance floor while Emilia orders a drink. I never deviate from my scotch, so I trust it'll be taken care of as I assess our surroundings. It's still early in the evening, but already the floor is full of writhing bodies belonging to people who want to forget for a little while. Forget what? It doesn't matter. Wanting to escape is one of the few truly universal human experiences, and people like me provide that escape at a nice markup.

The perky blonde girl brings us our drinks, and we toast silently. Emilia's eyes glow when they meet mine, though I notice how they shift back and forth as if the attention her presence earns makes her uncomfortable. It'll take time for her to get used to it. I trust she will. She can do anything.

I've taken a deep, warming sip from my glass before Emilia's frantic tugging at my sleeve steals my attention. "Oh my God," she shouts over the music, staring past me toward the VIP area. "Is that who I think it is?"

I look over her head to find a few NFL players seated there. Considering the activity around their table, they're feeling very generous with their money tonight. "Looks like it," I confirm, grinning down into her shining, flushed face. "I didn't know you followed football."

"Are you kidding? These guys are all over the place... TV, interviews, articles." I never took her for someone who'd care about celebrities, but then I suppose there will always be a moment of weak-kneed excitement over encountering athletes with Hall of Fame potential.

"You want to meet them?" I'm already tugging her along with me, enjoying how she stammers and blushes. "Hey, this is what they call a fringe benefit. Enjoy it," I urge with a grin.

Two of the guys sit a little straighter on our approach, and the recognition in their expressions tells me they've done their research. They know who owns this place and that I'm due the sort of respect they normally have heaped on them by low-level, sniveling assholes thrilled to death that such big names would grace their establishment.

That's not to say I'm blasé about the whole thing. "Whatever you gentlemen want tonight, it's on the house," I tell them, shaking my head and waving my hands when they protest. "I insist. It's a pleasure having you here."

That's how I feel until I notice the third member of their group and the way his attention has fallen on the woman at my side. He jerks his chin at her and crooks a finger from where he's seated in the booth. "Why don't you hang out here with me?" he asks, flashing a bright smile and reaching out, running his hand down her arm.

The room goes red as suddenly as if someone had flipped a switch. There's a roaring in my ears like that from

an approaching train as I nudge a silent Emilia aside. "Out!"
I bark. "Get your ass out of here and never come back. Go,
or I'll break your fucking neck."

"Whoa, whoa!" The other guys try to laugh it off. One of
them makes the mistake of clapping a hand over my shoulder, which I quickly throw off, glaring at him until he backs
down.

Turning back to the booth, I thrust an arm toward the
door. "I'll have you thrown out on your ass if you don't go on
your own. Make your choice, fucker."

He shoves his large frame out of the booth, glaring at
me. I'm guessing this is supposed to be threatening, like I'm
going to suddenly remember who I'm dealing with when he
unfolds his body and stands a head taller than me and probably sixty pounds heavier, at least. "You know who I am? You
know who I play for?" he demands with a scowl while his
buddies try to get him moving. They understand the danger
they're flirting with. He might not know whose club he's in,
but they do.

"I don't give a fuck who you play for." I snarl in his face.
"You get the fuck out of here and take your fucking friends
with you and never come back. Understood? I never wanna
see your face again." A face that falls slightly when Vinny
joins us, snarling in a silent invitation to fuck around and
find out.

His friends are smart enough to pull him away but not
smart enough to refrain from shooting filthy remarks as
they go. Not that I give a shit. One of the privileges of
running a business is deciding who we will serve. While I'm
sure my brother would give me shit if he heard about this,
it's my club.

I make the decisions.

Through all of this, Emilia has remained silent. I turn to

her, breathing heavily, and the look of wide-eyed surprise she wears does nothing but pour fuel over the flames of possessiveness already consuming me. I don't say a word. There's nothing to be said as I lead her back to the office, ignoring spectators still gathered around us. Let them watch. I can't bring myself to care about any of it. All that matters is getting her alone, now, before I explode. Vinny is smart enough to stay behind to stand guard, and I lock the door behind us, pounding my fist against the wood.

"Luca?" Her voice is small, trembling, full of questions.

"He touched you," I growl out. The mere memory leaves me punching the door again. "He thought you were some whore he could touch."

"I'm fine. We're fine." She places a hand on my shoulder. I know it's supposed to provide comfort, but it only serves as a reminder of what is mine. No one else's. Something erupts in me, something dark and vengeful. Something that gives me no choice but to take hold of her and push her against the door.

Her eyes snap open wide as she gasps, but the sound is cut off when I thrust my tongue into her mouth, invading her until she moans and melts against me as she always does.

My woman.

My everything.

I would swear an animal roars in my head, the sound of triumph, as I run a hand over her tits reaching between us, then pulling the dress up to her waist. One sharp tug and her panties give way, leaving her gasping in surprise before I cup her hot, plump mound. "This is mine," I growl out through clenched teeth, staring into her bulging eyes. Eyes that quickly darken with need and understanding. "Say it," I demand, my hold on her firm and unrelenting.

"Yours." She reaches down to grasp my ass, pulling me in, demanding all of me. "Yours."

I'm helpless in the face of this overwhelming, all-consuming heat. Sliding my fingers through Emilia's silky wetness makes her gasp, nails digging into my shoulders hard enough that I feel the pressure through my jacket and shirt. She rocks her hips against my hand, then bears down on my fingers, practically forcing them inside her. It's with a chuckle that I give her what she wants, fucking her with them, grinding my covered cock against her hip while the wet, sloppy sounds of her arousal fill the air.

Only I can do this to her.

Only I can make her whimper and beg.

I can turn her into this gasping, needy thing.

"Fuck me," she begs, now clutching the back of my neck and pulling my face close, brushing her lips against mine and moaning into my mouth. "Give it to me. I need your cock inside me."

My cock aches painfully in response, and she doesn't need to say another word. I pull back far enough to drop my pants, my hands trembling with need, my desperation leaving me grunting in frustration when I can't get inside her fast enough.

When it comes to her, there is no fast enough.

As soon as I'm free of the confines of my pants, dripping in anticipation, Emilia wraps her fingers around me and strokes my hardened length. Then, without hesitation, she guides me into her, spreading her legs, draping one over my hip, and drawing me in.

My knees practically buckle at the first stroke inside her quivering sheath—so tight, so greedy for me. I drive myself deep, hard enough to rattle the door, but all she does is smile and narrow her blue eyes as if accepting a challenge. "That's right," she whispers, running her hands over me, raking them through my hair, down my back, and dragging her nails across my ass. "Give it to me. Make me yours."

Then her eyes close, and a deep moan fills my ears as I drive into her again and again against the door, crushing her between it and my body, claiming her with every stroke, taking what's mine, tasting her skin when she throws back her head in abandon, lapping at her throat while she holds me close, whispering in my ear.

"Fuck me," she rasps between sharp, strained breaths. "Fuck me hard. I'm all yours, Luca."

Mine.

She's mine.

There's nothing in the world powerful enough to change that. Not my family, her job, not some hotshot football player who thinks an eight-figure contract gives him carte blanche to do and say whatever he wants. The door rattles, and her high-pitched whimpers build in volume with every sure, deep thrust until her muscles clamp down around me.

"Oh... oh, shit... I'm going to come..." Her breath catches as she clenches around me.

Hearing the words tumble from her parted lips starts the telltale tingle at the base of my spine, which quickly spreads through my core. "Come on my cock," I grunt out, trying to hold back for her sake but losing ground. "Be my good girl."

She opens her eyes and stares into mine, silently daring me to look away. I can't. I won't. I watch her through every moment of the orgasm sweeping over her all at once, the tightening of her muscles pushing me over the edge. I thrust into her, needing to be deeper, filling her while she clings to me, trembling, gasping for air in the aftermath.

I'm never as vulnerable as I am at this moment. Shaking

the way she does, ears ringing, and heart pounding, this woman owns me. I would stop at nothing for her.

"I love you," she whispers in my ear between shuddering breaths, and the words are balm for my troubled soul as we navigate the aftermath together, slumped against the door while a party rages on the other side.

5

EMILIA

I need to do something.

I've been here two weeks and feel no more comfortable walking along the flagstone path leading up to the main house. There's no universe in which Dante isn't still resentful over my presence, and I'm not about to rub that in his face. Not that I'd do so purposely, not in a million years. Though, I'm sure he sees it that way.

The look of complete disgust and cold hatred he wore while the men of the family decided my fate isn't something I'll ever forget.

Then again, what would I do up there that I can't do here? There's a gym in the basement and the in-home movie theater, but neither of those activities will fill my entire day. That's what I need—something to fill my time.

Taking care of the house certainly isn't enough to make my days feel full and worthwhile. It doesn't take very long, for one thing. Having been built for Luca alone, there isn't a lot of space as luxurious as it is. For another, Luca spends most of his time up at the house, working with his dad and brother, making sure they aren't vulnerable and have enough manpower at their various businesses to keep things secure. He isn't around long enough to make much of a mess.

That's where he is now. I can picture him up there, in the study, glaring at his brother over the top of their father's head as they both practically kill themselves, trying to earn the old man's respect. Sibling rivalry—a tale as old as time. I hum the Disney tune to myself as I begin stripping the bed and wonder which of the sons is the beauty and which is the beast. I doubt either of them would find my observation humorous.

How does Isabella deal with the loneliness? I guess it was different for her back in the day. She had children to take care of and a big house to run. Nowadays, she still has plenty of people coming in and out, plenty to manage.

I have a few rooms to dust and vacuum, and I only do that because I see no point in having a housekeeper like Dante does in his house on the other end of the property. *His time is too valuable to be wasted washing dishes.*

The thought makes me roll my eyes once I've finished changing the sheets and throwing the dirty set in the wash along with towels. There it is—the big activity of my day. I used to work insane hours, pouring myself into research, interviews, and tracking down leads. My work was my life. I was exhausted, but I loved it.

What's my life now? What does my future look like? I have the big picture settled. I'll be with Luca, a thought that fills me with warmth and satisfaction. My soul recognized his the night we met, but my brain had a hard time catching up to the inevitable.

But the everyday stuff is still foggy and unfocused. Do I go back to school? Maybe, but what would I study? Will there ever come a time when I have the freedom to come and go as I please? What about marriage, a family? I want all of it. I wish I knew when to expect it or how to blend my new family with the family who believes I'm still a detective.

A sudden buzzing startles me in the otherwise silent house while I put new sheets on the bed. One glance at the screen turns my blood to ice since I was wondering how to explain any of this to my parents. It's one thing to imagine happiness, love, and babies, but another to imagine my parents accepting my choice.

No way. I'm imagining this. It's way too soon for her to be calling. Yet the thought of something terribly wrong with my parents, who are supposed to be in Outback Australia now and out of touch until they get home, forces me to answer the call.

"Mom?" I whisper since that's the best I can do with my throat so tight and my mouth suddenly dry as a bone. She's not supposed to be able to get in touch with me. This is all wrong. I'm not prepared to introduce her to my new life.

Her broken cry makes me wince, not only because it's loud enough to make my ears ring. "Oh, thank goodness! There I was, imagining the worst! You're all right, aren't you? You're not hurt or anything? You didn't move and not tell me? What happened while we were gone?"

As usual, I'm left confused by my mother's rapid-fire questions. She has a way of weaving them into a thick blanket heavy enough to drag me down and rob me of the will to live. Considering I wasn't expecting to hear from her for weeks, I'm more dazed than ever. "Hang on a second," I counter when I find my voice. "Where are you?"

"I'm standing in your apartment, and it looks like you've been robbed!" Her voice is shaky, full of raw emotion.

I drop to the bed when my legs start shaking too hard to hold me up. No fucking way. This is not happening. Of all the possible roadblocks and challenges I've pondered over in the two weeks since I came to live here on the Santoro compound, my parents never came into the equation. I've been happy to brush them aside since they were supposed to be overseas for another three weeks.

"What do you mean you're in my apartment?" I demand when the shock wears off enough for anger to seep into my voice. "Since when do you show up unannounced?"

"Since when do I need a reason to surprise my daughter? I thought you'd be happy to see us home so soon," she insists. As always, she's the victim, hurt by my lack of enthusiasm. The woman is a pro at turning any situation into an opportunity to be the wounded party.

There are much more pressing questions fighting for the chance to be a voice, and I blurt out the biggest one of all rather than explain myself, "Why did you come home so early, anyway? Are you guys okay?" I wouldn't put it past her to give me shit about the apartment while forgetting to mention Dad is sick or something. I love the woman, but knowing we're both on the same continent again is enough to make my insides feel hot and queasy.

"That's not important now!" I hear her voice bounce off the walls and can picture her standing in the living room, throwing her hands into the air in a familiar gesture. "Where is everything? All the pictures on the walls are gone. Your books are off the shelves. What goes on around here? We go on vacation, and you decide to move?"

Deep breaths. If I get overly agitated all too fast, she'll take it as a sign that things are terrible and I need her to jump in. "Everything is fine," I announce in a quieter voice. I wish it felt closer to the truth. But the icy sweat now dampening the nape of my neck tells another story. I'm not ready for this.

"So where is everything? You're not making sense, Emilia Jane."

Everybody knows it's serious when the full name comes out. I'm twenty-four years old, but twenty years are magically shaved off my age when I hear it. "I have my reasons. I can't share them just yet. Trust me when I tell you everything is fine. I'm not in any danger, I'm not sick, and nobody robbed me. Nothing is wrong."

She scoffs loudly, making me wince again. "Well, I find it hard to believe they could be anything that would warrant you moving half the things from your apartment."

My jaw hurts from clenching so tight. "I can tell you all about it eventually, just not right now. I'm sorry. I know how that sounds."

"I don't like this. Neither will your father when I tell him."

"Speaking of Dad, is he all right? You didn't say why you guys came back so early." I need to distract her. We have to get off this topic and fast.

"Oh, that." She sounds disgusted, which doesn't bode well. "There was a big mix-up with the company we booked through, and they messed up our arrangements and ended up double booking our hotel when we got to the third stop on the tour. Since everything was nonrefundable, we couldn't recoup our losses. We could've gone somewhere else and put it on a card, but your dad was so angry, he didn't feel like staying."

And that's my father in a nutshell. Why blame the travel company when you can blame an entire country? The equivalent of taking his ball and going home. "That's awful. I'm sorry it ended so soon."

"Oh, I don't know," she says with a light, breezy sigh. "These things happen for a reason."

"Did you not enjoy it out there?" *Please, tell me all about it.* Every single detail, so long as we don't delve deeper into my current living situation.

"This was always much more your father's idea than mine. I went along with it because that's what you do when you're married." She always finds a way to make herself sound like a martyr. "So we had to cut the trip short. Good thing we got insurance on our flight, or else we would be stuck out there in that stifling heat with your dad in a lousy mood. I shudder to think."

"Me too."

"So, where are you? At the station? I could come over. We could go for lunch later."

Out of everything she's said so far, that's what sets the red flags waving in my head. "No, don't do that. I'm not at the station. I'm..." There's only one way to get past this without her finding out anything before I'm ready to open up. "I sort of can't talk about it right now. If anything, I probably shouldn't have answered your call, but I wanted to be sure there weren't any emergencies or whatever." I squeeze my eyes shut, praying she'll buy it.

If there is a hell, I'm probably going there for lying like this. Good thing I don't believe in it. I've seen too much of the hell humans can create for each other to believe there's anything in the afterlife that could be worse.

My admission has the intended effect. "Oh my goodness!" she says with a gasp. "Please go. Don't endanger yourself on my account."

"It's not that serious," I insist with a soft laugh. I don't need my mom giving herself a stroke. "But I am very busy. And I should go, but I will get back to you soon. I promise." Another lie. I'm buying time to come up with a plausible excuse.

"Tell me you're being safe," she pleads. "That whatever you're doing, you aren't in any danger."

I respond the only way I can, the only way I ever have since graduating from the academy and working my way up. "I'll do my best. Love to Dad." And I end the call before my guilt can consume me. It's only when I'm staring at my darkened phone that I remember wanting to ask when she got in the habit of entering my apartment without warning. Is this the first time? Somehow, I doubt it.

There's only so long I'll be able to dodge my parents now that they're back in town. Eventually, I will have to tell them everything about Luca and me. This isn't some fling that will fizzle out after some time. All I have to do now is figure out how to make the rest of my life fit into my plans.

My hand trembles as I set the phone down and pace the room. Like I don't have enough on my mind, the prospect of breaking the news to my parents has been moved up three weeks. I have to figure out a way to not only confess I've resigned from the department without shocking them to death but that I'm in love with the son of a notorious mob boss whose family was in my crosshairs until not so long ago. Then I have to convince them to keep things under wraps, or else risk word of my relationship getting back to my former superiors and possibly getting me into an even bigger mess when my lies are uncovered. Not only me but the family now sheltering me.

And I was fretting over not having enough to do.

6

LUCA

I know who's inside.

Standing at the window of my father's study, I can see my house. What is she doing? All I want is for her to relax, get comfortable, and make herself at home. She's my world now. Every minute I spend away from her is spent counting the seconds until we're together again. It leaves me edgy and impatient. And patience was never one of my virtues in the first place.

"I'm sorry..." My brother's voice rings out behind me, just as sharp as the crack of a whip. That's what he thinks he's doing. Whipping me. "Are we interrupting your daydreaming by talking about business?"

"I'm sorry," I counter, looking over my shoulder to where my brother glares at me from a chair in front of Papa's desk. Like the kid who always has to sit in the front row so the teacher knows they're paying attention. He might as well bring a polished apple to leave on the desk—insufferable ass-kisser. "I've been staring at your ugly face for hours and thought I would try for a change of scenery. What was I thinking?" I ask as I return his glare.

"All right, that's enough," Papa murmurs, shaking his head. "I swear, the two of you never stop. We are all under the gun here. We don't need to pick fights among ourselves and make things worse."

He makes perfect sense, but he never had a brother like Dante. Uncle Tomasso was so much like my father. They were practically interchangeable, nearly identical in appearance, right down to how their stomachs started to go paunchy in middle age. Their voices were close enough that I couldn't tell them apart over the phone, and they shared the same booming laugh and a sense of humor to go with it. I was positive they had to be twins during my childhood, and I was stunned when I found out otherwise.

It was easy for them to get along, as alike as they were. Dante and me, on the other hand? There have been times when I've considered getting our DNA tested to confirm we have the same parents.

Dante clears his throat and jumps in before I can speak a word in my defense. "All right. Today, we confirmed the Accardi and Marino families are still backing us and are squeezing Vitali out of sports booking in the other four boroughs. Antonio and the crew back in Sicily promised additional soldiers whenever we need them."

"Let's keep that in our back pocket," Papa decides as he leans back in his chair with a weary sigh. "We can have them here within a day once we send word we need them. There's no sense in calling them too soon." He opens the top two buttons of his shirt, releasing a shaky breath. A glance in Dante's direction tells me he doesn't notice. He's too busy taking notes.

Papa is close enough that I reach out and place a hand on his shoulder. The faint smile I get in return is only a shadow of his normal self. His pallor is gray and sickly, while dark circles stand out under his eyes. I know better than to jump to conclusions, especially when it comes to someone like my father. He won't be babied or coddled, and it's easy for him to mistake concern for being treated like a child. It's his pride.

I can't pretend I don't relate, but it's damn frustrating when I'm standing on the outside, looking in. Should I ask if he's feeling well? Maybe he won't give me any answers, but Mama will if I ask the right way. I'm starting to think the time has come for me to do that. What's the alternative? Standing around and watching him slowly fade away?

It feels traitorous to entertain a thought like that, but facts are facts. I've watched him more closely ever since that first dinner after Emilia moved in, and his condition only seems to have gotten worse in the two weeks since then. That I'm thinking of it as a condition makes me feel sick and uneasy. I hope I'm wrong.

For once in my life, I want to be wrong.

"Sicily offered a fresh influx of cash," Dante continues. "Whatever we need."

"We shouldn't need it." Papa looks my way like he's checking for confirmation, and I nod firmly. "We're in good shape last I checked the books. And there's still the stockpile of weapons and ammo at our warehouse in Queens, so that's settled."

"I double-checked the security detail we've set up there," I interject, hoping to comfort him. "Everything is running smoothly."

The look of relief that touches his face turns to irritation when Dante snorts. "Wow. Congratulations. You managed to make a phone call." His sour smirk is the perfect punctuation mark, one I'd love to wipe off his face.

"What the fuck is your problem?" I demand, ignoring

my father's quiet groan of dismay in favor of marching around the desk and standing in front of my brother with my feet planted and my fists clenched. "Are we in this together, or aren't we?"

He has the audacity to blink as he tilts his head back to look up at me, like he's innocent or somehow confused. "Why would we not be in this together?" he asks with a sickening smile.

"Boys, enough of this," Papa murmurs.

But that's the thing. I *have* had enough, and I'm still ingesting my brother's shit. All for the sake of keeping the peace and maintaining a united front in this most dangerous time. I'm doing everything I can, yet he insists on heaping more of his shit on my plate at every opportunity.

"When are you going to grow up?" I ask him, tipping my head to the side. "Honestly. When will you learn to accept defeat gracefully?"

"That depends," he tells me, still smiling with those same hard eyes. "I haven't been defeated yet."

All I can do is bark out a laugh. "Right. I didn't know you were a comedian."

That gets him. His face darkens while his nostrils flare, and now I know he's taking the gloves off. Good. I'd rather lay everything out bare than dance around his obvious resentment. "Listen up." He snarls. "You can keep your little slut here—"

My breath catches. "Shut your fucking mouth!"

"But don't expect me to be happy about it," he continues, ignoring me. "I'm not going to sit here, pretending I agree with it, and I won't pretend the extra work you've heaped on all of us—"

"I said enough!" Papa slams his hands against the desk, jumping from his chair and growling at both of us. Now he's

the man I grew up loving and fearing and equal parts, practically on fire, ready to rip our heads off. "I am sick to death
of listening to the two of you bickering like a couple of children! Dammit, this didn't only happen because of that girl,
Dante," he barks out.

Before I can gloat a little, he whirls on me. "It didn't
make things better, though. How the hell am I supposed to
leave this family to my sons when my sons can't stop
bitching at each other long enough to run it?"

Dante clears his throat, sets his tablet aside, then stands.
"Papa, it's—"

"Did I ask you to speak?" he snaps, loud enough for both
of us to flinch. A deep red flush has crept up his neck and
now floods his cheeks. "I can't rest easy with the two of you
at each other's goddamn throats all the time! When are you
going to grow up and put this rivalry shit behind you? What
is it going to take?"

As he asks the question, he sways slightly, then leans his
weight on his hands. "Oh... oh, fuck..."

"Papa?" I yell, but his eyes flutter, and he drops to the
floor.

"Get help!" Dante practically vaults over the desk to get
to him while I run across the room and fling open the door.

"Get in here!" I bark at the guards. Returning to the
desk, my father lies on the floor, appearing unconscious.

"Papa, Papa, hang in there. Take it easy." Dante presses
an ear to his chest, and I notice the way he grips our father's
shirt in his fist before releasing a sigh. "He's breathing. He
has a steady heartbeat."

My relief is short-lived. Just because Papa is still
breathing and his heart is beating doesn't mean he's all
right. "We should get him to his room," I decide, and with
the help of the guards, we manage to get him on his feet

with his arms draped over our shoulders, half-walk, half-dragging him to the hall. He's barely conscious, mumbling something I can't understand while his chin touches his chest.

"Save your strength," I urge him, but that's a selfish request. I don't want him to wear himself out, but how he's mumbling incoherently is like an icy hand gripping my heart. This is not my father. My father does not fall apart like this. He's still got years to go. We aren't ready to lose him.

I don't know whether Dante is thinking along the lines I am as we carry our father between us, but I doubt it. We've never shared much when it comes to the way our minds work, so why would that change now? At least we're working together to get Papa up the stairs with the guards behind us, ready to catch him if he drops.

"Stay with us," I beg as we trek down a hallway that has never seemed so long after reaching the top of the stairs. "You need to rest, that's all. You've been working too hard." Dante grunts but is smart enough to keep his thoughts to himself. If anything, this would be the moment to unload on me since what am I going to do with Papa leaning against me as we fight to get him to his bed?

"What is all the commotion?" My mother's question is answered when she reaches the hallway and sees us practically carrying Papa. "*Amore mio, sei malato?*" <Are you ill, my love?>

"He passed out," I tell her before Dante can turn this into my fault. It very well could be. I might've sent him over the edge by bringing Emilia home. No, I can't allow myself to entertain that idea, and I push it out of my mind while Mama hurries into the bedroom and turns down the bedding so we can make him more comfortable.

"He's been working too hard," Mama announces, jumping into action as soon as we've set him on the bed.

Time has slowed her down a little, and on a rainy day like this one, she would move slower, thanks to the knee she broke years ago, the damp weather irritating it. Yet she moves with the speed of someone Guilia's age, dropping to her knees and removing his shoes, then standing again to unbutton his shirt before helping him stretch out on his back.

"Now tell me exactly how this started," she demands, fixing the pillows behind his head and propping him up.

"I can tell you where it started," Dante offers. When I look at him, he's staring at me with rage burning in his familiar eyes. Eyes so much like my own, it's unnerving at times. "It's been about, what? Three weeks, maybe four, since you decided to go rogue and forget the family and hideout in the cabin?"

"Luca!" Mama shouts when I cock my fist back without thinking. My brother's head snaps back, but he doesn't flinch. Either he's too stunned I'd make a move like that in front of our parents, or he knows I wouldn't go through with it.

I would've let my fist piston forward to connect with anything I could hit if we were alone. But once I got started, I don't know if I would have been able to stop. Instead, I stop myself at the last second and remember who's standing beside me.

"Don't you dare," our mother whispers in horror as she takes me by the wrist and lowers my arm. "Don't you ever let me see you do that again. Either of you."

In the same breath, she whirls on Dante. "As for you, don't you ever let me hear you say anything like that about your brother again. I don't expect you two to get along all

the time, but dammit, you are brothers. Blood. The future of
this family depends on both of you, and unless you provide
a solid foundation, it *will* crumble. You're too old for me to
put you over my knee and give you the spanking you
deserve, but you are pushing me."

"Mi amore," Papa whispers. It's the first coherent thing
he's managed since he collapsed. He lifts a hand, motioning
for her to join him.

"What happened?" Now she's the loving wife, stroking
hair away from his forehead once she's sitting on the edge of
the bed, offering him water from the pitcher he keeps on his
nightstand. He sips it slowly, looking up at her with pure
love and trust radiating from his eyes.

"I got dizzy," he murmurs, then slowly turns his gaze
toward Dante and me. "Forgive me, boys. I didn't mean to
frighten you."

"Don't worry about it." Dante's voice is warmer than I've
heard in a long time as he offers Papa a reassuring smile that
never quite reaches his eyes. They're still hard. Whether
that's because of me or because he understands how serious
this could be, I don't know. I doubt he'd tell me if I asked.
"You get your rest now. I'll head downstairs and keep things
in order. Don't worry about a thing."

He manages to throw a threatening look at me as he
turns away from the foot of the bed, one I pretend not to
notice. His bullshit isn't important now. Rather than stew
over him, I lower the blinds and close the curtains over
them so Papa can sleep. "Dante's right," I tell him as I go
from one window to the other. "You have nothing to worry
about except resting and feeling better."

"Thank you, son," he replies in a weak voice. "I feel
better already."

I wish that were true, and the sort of well-meaning platitudes Papa used to offer when I was a kid made a difference now when I'm too old to believe them. Mama murmurs a few loving words, joining me in the hallway so he can sleep in peace.

Once the door is closed, I turn to her. "Tell me the truth," I whisper, taking her by the hands and noticing how they tremble. "What's wrong with him? Is he sick? What can we do?"

Her loving blue eyes meet mine, full of hesitation. Maybe fear. Yet, for the first time I'm aware of, the most honest person I've ever known lies straight to my face. "He'll be fine," she whispers, mustering a shaky smile. "He's overly tired, is all."

7

EMILIA

"I am so sick of all this war stuff already!" Guilia throws her arms out to her sides, staring up at the clear, blue sky in the middle of our walk around the property, staying close to the wall, always within the eyesight of a guard.

Is this what it feels like to be a celebrity, constantly swarmed by fans and paparazzi? The thought makes my skin crawl.

I look toward the closest guard once Guilia finishes shouting, but he doesn't seem to care. She can scream in frustration, but if she starts screaming in pain or fear, it's clear he will step in.

"What is it usually like around here?" I ask since I've wanted to know about that for weeks. Hell, even longer than that, back to when I first became involved in investigating the Santoro crime family. The question wasn't specific to their family, of course. Just how do you live in the world when your family has shed so much blood? How do you exist alongside other people?

"There are always guards," she quickly explains. "You

get used to that. I mean, I don't think I can remember a time when I didn't have guys watching me."

"Even at school?" I figured Rocco was protective, but that sounds like overkill. He would know whether she was in danger, though.

"They took me to and from most days," she explains. "And they always waited outside the school. I think they worked in shifts. Somebody always had an eye on the building." I can't tell from her matter-of-fact description how she felt about it. I guess if that's all you know, the way you grew up, you can't really appreciate how different you are. Then again, she must've known. Even if she attended an expensive private school, those kids couldn't have grown up as she did. Kids must have given her funny looks over the guards. Growing up like that can't be easy, yet she seems remarkably well-adjusted.

She kicks a rock and sighs. "But at least I could go places and do things."

"So security isn't always this tight?" I ask.

Her dark curls bounce when she shakes her head. "God, no. I would go crazy if it was. I'm going crazy as it is right now."

"It won't be forever." I hope. It's the sort of thing you say when you're completely unsure of yourself.

"You're right," she agrees. "It just feels that way."

I can't help but laugh, though it's gentle. Guilia grins when I sling an arm around her shoulders and hug her. "I know I've said it before, but I'm so glad you're here. It was so lame, being the only girl," she confesses as we continue wearing a path in the lawn.

"It does sound kind of lame," I agree.

"You said you were the only kid in your family, right?" I nod, and her face takes on a wistful expression. "Sometimes

I've wished I was the only child. I love my brothers, but they are a little much. That's how they're supposed to be." She narrows her eyes in an impression of her father's customary scowl. "Boys are supposed to be loud and assertive," she grunts out in a voice not unlike his.

"Not so for girls?" I ask, though I know the answer.

"Between you and me, I think he likes it when I give him a little bit of shit. I keep him on his toes." When I think back on how fondly he always looks at her, I can imagine she's right. She's certainly his princess.

"Is that how it is with your dad?" she asks, wincing. "Sorry. I shouldn't assume your dad is around or whatever. Or maybe it's a sore subject."

"It's not a sore subject," I insist. "My dad and I have a good relationship. He was always working when I was little, though, so I'm closer to my mom." Closer, but not exactly close. Guilia doesn't need to hear the entire story. I'm sure I'd bore her with it, anyway.

"What does he do?" she asks.

I wince, unable to stop it. "He's a lawyer."

Her full lips twitch. "Is he the kind of lawyer my family would use?" Something in my expression makes her laugh, interrupting my attempt to come up with a diplomatic response. "I'm sorry. I couldn't help it. I'm only teasing," she adds with a tiny giggle.

"He's not your family's kind of lawyer," I settle for saying.

"What did he think about you resigning?"

What an interesting question. I don't know what to say since she's asking me about something that hasn't happened yet. "I—"

"Guilia!" At the sound of Isabella's voice, we both turn. She's standing on the back terrace, wrapping her cardigan tighter around her shivering body. "Lunch!"

"Eighteen years old, and I still have to eat on a schedule," Guilia mutters while I smile and wave at her mom. She shoots me a hopeful look. "Will you come with me? You know Mama would love it if you had lunch with us."

I would like to. I wish I could. Spending more time with the women around here would be nice since they've never done anything but make me feel welcome. I know it would make Luca happy, too, finding I spent time with them.

He could use some good news, and lunch with the ladies might perk him up.

Things have been even more strained these past few days since Rocco had some sort of attack. Luca doesn't know for sure what caused it, but he has his suspicions. It's eating him up inside to think his father could be sick, but he doesn't want to admit it.

It's the thought of Dante that makes me shake my head. "You know how it is. I don't want to cause any trouble."

"Dante's the one causing trouble," she reminds me, narrowing her brown eyes. "You shouldn't have to suffer for it."

"I'm not suffering." I give her a gentle shove in the direction of the house, and she sighs, shaking her head and mumbling something that sounds pretty hateful before crossing the wide lawn and jogging up the steps to the terrace. Isabella wraps an arm around her waist, and they walk into the house together while I watch, wishing I could have something resembling an honest, open relationship with my mother.

Rather than return to the little house, I continue walking, admiring the grounds I've wandered countless times. Of course, I understand things won't always be like this, but I'm with Guilia. I can't wait for this to be over. Maybe Dante will loosen up a little bit, too, and I won't have to feel quite so much like the enemy.

It's funny, Guilia mentioning my family and asking questions. They've been on my mind lately, and not only because Mom still texts every day, like this morning's text, which came through while I was in the shower.

Mom: *Please tell me you're being safe. It's driving me to distraction, not knowing.*

I sent her a thumbs-up emoji and waited for a barrage of follow-up questions, but they never came. Thank God for small favors.

I'm pretty sure my current guard's name is Pete. I almost want to ask if he'd have lunch with me. He's probably not much of a conversationalist, but at least I wouldn't be alone. I've never been anybody's idea of a social butterfly, but in my old life, I could reach out to friends and see them if I felt up to it. I can't do that now.

Someday, when things calm down.

A cold wind blows my hair back and makes me duck my chin, rubbing my arms briskly. It's time to head inside for something hot to drink.

The sight of a man dressed in dark gray slacks and a black button-down makes my heart skip a beat. He's on his way down from the main house with a plastic container in one hand. By the time I round the gardens between the two structures, the midday sun makes his black hair gleam, and his wide smile shines bright against his olive skin as I run to him.

"Hi!" I throw my arms around Luca's neck, and he catches me against him with his free arm. I'll never get tired of the feel of his firm body and the musky scent of his favorite cologne. Some mornings, when he gets out of bed before I do, I make it a point to inhale the scent that lingers on his pillow.

"Hey, you." Luca nuzzles my neck, and I groan happily at his warm breath touching my cold skin. "Sitting through hours of Dante's bullshit is worth it when this is my reward."

I would normally shy away from a kiss outside the house, just in case somebody is watching— somebody who doesn't approve. Yet I can't bring myself to care this particular afternoon, and he groans as I enthusiastically return the kiss. "Fuck, you're in a good mood," he growls out when I let him up for air.

"Thanks to you," I purr. He's the reason I'm going through all of this—the scrutiny, the sense of always being watched and judged, fearing for my life—it's all for him. When I'm close to him like this, he helps me remember there's something bigger at stake.

"Mama sent me down with lasagna for lunch," he explains, squeezing me before letting go so we can make it inside. "She said there's enough for an army, and you are entirely too thin. Her exact words."

"What are *your* exact words?" I counter when we're in the house and away from prying eyes, dropping my coat once he's set the container down. Lasagna isn't going to satisfy my hunger, not when he's with me.

His dark eyes twinkle with understanding as he takes me by the hips and yanks me against him. "I like your body the way it is," he growls out, his fingers pressing against my flesh. "Though, I wouldn't complain if you got a little curvier. More to hold onto." To emphasize his point, he squeezes me, pulling me closer.

"Luca Santoro," I whisper as I wind my arms around his neck. "In many ways, you are the perfect man. Now take me to bed so we can work up an appetite."

8

LUCA

There's a wild animal in my office, and for once, it isn't me.

I can only sit here and pretend not to notice Emilia's restless attitude for so long. In the hours since we arrived at the club, she's picked up and discarded a book, played a game on her phone before setting it aside, then picked up the book again only to start pacing the room, meandering, and it's beginning to wear on my nerves.

I'd rather have her here than be without her. Yet there's no trace of the happy, upbeat energy from her first visit last week—though she insisted she wanted to come along this evening.

Thanks to my work, we spend so much time apart, and she wants to be with me whenever possible. I didn't see anything wrong with the idea, barring one important point —I don't want her out in the club without me. I don't want her exposed to the eyes and hands of the shitheads who are good enough to give me their money but nowhere near good enough to be in her presence.

Finally, after double-checking our purchase orders for the upcoming weeks, I lower the lid to my MacBook and watch her wander around the office. "What's on your mind?" I ask, watching each pass she makes without her noticing I've turned my full attention her way. She's that distracted and distant.

Emilia turns, her brows lifting like she's shocked by my question, as if she is so good at hiding her feelings. Even if she was, she should know by now that I can see through her. "Nothing," she insists, and her voice is much too chipper to be believable. "I'm fine."

"Are you? Because it looks like you're going to wear a hole in the floor. You should have one of those step counter things. I'd be interested to know how far you've walked already tonight." I make sure to smile so she knows I'm not pissed or irritated. I'm more concerned if anything.

"Sorry. I guess I just don't have anything to do, really. I want to be with you," she insists in a rush when my brows draw together. "That's why I'm here. I want us to be together as much as we can." Her teeth sink into her lip before she averts her gaze.

"But you're bored," I finish for her.

"That sounds harsh. I'm not trying to be," Emilia insists, wrinkling her nose.

"I know." Folding my hands over my stomach, I take her in. Gone is the de la Renta from Saks. She's still hot as hell in tight jeans and an off-the-shoulder sweater that leaves me longing to run my lips over her skin. If anything, I like her better this way, especially in public. There's no making her unattractive, but she's not asking for attention. Only I get to enjoy her body. "You're too good to me to be harsh."

A soft smile touches her glossy lips. It's a shame she's feeling so anxious, or I'd suggest putting those lips to work. I can't help it. She has that effect on me. "That's sweet of you to say, but I don't know. Lately, I feel like I'm a lot of trouble. I'm supposed to be adding to your life, right? All I'm doing is raising issues and complaining."

"You feel directionless. That's not a complaint. And listen..." I motion for her to come to me, and she does without hesitating, crossing the room and propping her ass on the edge of the desk so she's between my spread legs. I could suggest ways for her to keep herself occupied while she's here, but that would only be a quick diversion. The underlying issue would still exist. "I know I'm not great at this whole talking about our feelings thing, but I'm trying. I'm in this forever, and that means I'm responsible for you having everything you need. If you need something and I'm not providing it, I have to know."

She draws a deep breath, then blows it out. "I don't want to hurt your feelings," she whispers.

Not exactly a great start. "I understand," I murmur as evenly as I can. This is so new to me. I want to be the man she needs, but this is my first time in this position. I'm vulnerable, and it has never been something I've adjusted to very well. The woman sitting in front of me holds my life in her hands—nothing short of that. It's uncomfortable. The uncertainty is enough to make me scream as she fights to find the words.

"It's just that I feel like the walls are closing in on me all the time," she admits in a soft voice. "I can't breathe. I'm always being watched. I have to stay on the grounds unless I'm at the club with you. It's a lot to deal with." She looks miserable by the time she's finished.

"You'll adjust," I offer. "It will take time. Give yourself a chance."

"Time?" She winces, and I know it was the wrong thing

to say. "And how much time would that be? I don't mean
with Vitali," she insists when I was about to mention the
name. "That's one thing. What I'm saying is, how much time
do you think it's going to take for me to adjust to my whole
life being changed all at once?"

What's gotten into her? This is all so abrupt. Maybe
when her parents are back in the country, she'll feel more
connected to her life outside the family. Until then, this is
my problem to deal with.

I notice her hands trembling while she picks nervously
at her nails. She's afraid, and that's the last thing I want. I
would never hurt her. Doesn't she know that by now? "My
life has changed too," I remind her in what I hope is a gentle
voice.

"Not the way mine has," she quickly counters, almost
like she was waiting for that argument and has her answer
prepared.

"You don't have to sound so sour about it," I mumble.
Heat rises in my core, flushing my skin, leaving me irritated
and floundering to understand. I want to give Emilia what
she needs, but how can I do that when she sounds so damn
accusatory?

The creases in her forehead deepen when she scowls.
"See? You tell me to share everything with you, and when I
do, you're angry."

"I'm not angry," I insist, which isn't technically a lie. But
I'm getting there.

"You're doing a pretty great impression of it, then." She
groans when I scoff. "Please, listen to me. Hear me. Your
life has changed. Yes. I won't take that from you. But it has
not changed as profoundly as mine, and you can't pretend
otherwise. I'm not only talking about my job," she insists
when I scoff again. "But let's not forget I was used to

coming and going as I pleased. I had my work. I had somewhere to go every day. I felt like I was doing something and contributing somehow. I called the shots, made my own choices, saw people, and interacted with the world. And now? I'm trying so hard to get used to this new reality, but every day, it's like I lose a little more ground and a bit of myself, and I don't know how to stop it. I love you and hope you would want to help me." By the time she's finished, her chest is heaving, and her eyes shine with unshed tears.

I don't know what part to focus on first. The last thing she said is the freshest, so I latch onto that. "Since when do I not want to help you?" I demand through gritted teeth.

She'll never know how hard I'm struggling to keep calm. There is no way she could comprehend the seething heat in my chest that I would normally vent with my fists or a gun. I can't use those outlets now. There's nothing to do but fight every violent impulse I possess.

She lowers her brow, staring at me for a silent beat. "Since you take this attitude with me," she replies, sounding confused. "I tell you I need something, and you take it as a personal insult."

"Who's insulted?" I challenge as I lean back in my chair, arms spread in a shrug. "I'm not. Maybe you're projecting."

"Don't do that," she mutters, shaking her head. "Don't try to gaslight me now."

The mention of that word makes my skin crawl. "I didn't think you were someone who used the buzzwords of the day to make a point. I gave you a little credit for being intelligent."

She flinches, and pain flares to life in her eyes. "Don't be mean. I'm coming to you with this, and you're throwing it back in my face. That's not how this is supposed to go." She folds her arms defensively and might as well rub salt in my wounds.

I hate myself for making her feel this way.

I hate myself more for not knowing how to fix it.

"Exactly how is it supposed to go?" I ask. "You're telling me I'm not enough for you. Am I supposed to be happy about that?"

"That is not at all what I'm saying! That's what you're taking from this? Fuck!" She throws her hands into the air and pushes away from the desk, but I'm quicker, standing and caging her in with an arm to either side of her body. "You're starting to have second thoughts, aren't you?" I lean in, forcing her to lean back a little. "That's what this is really about. That's what you don't want to say."

She blurts out a loud laugh. "What? Wrong. Dammit, you're completely wrong." There are no more tears. No more trembling. I forgot how hard she makes my cock when her temper flares. Part of me wants to see how far this will go. I could sink into her so deep she'd forget everything that's making her miserable.

Yet, she softens instead of blowing up the way I wish she would. Her head tips to the side, her mouth curves into a sad frown, and her hands touch the sides of my face. Normally, her touch is magic, but right now, it does nothing to soothe me. "Let's not do this," she whispers. "I don't want to fight."

It's too late. I am already consumed by a sense of helpless frustration that has intensified into something closer to rage. This is the last person I need to rage against, but she happens to be the only person in the room with me, the only one with this power over me. Even Dante isn't able to cut through me the way she does with a single look, a single word. Only she can expose me like she does. I'm a fucking fraud. I don't know the first thing about making another human being happy. It could be I'm not the man she needs.

Fuck that.

I'm not letting it end like this. "You're not the only person who's ever gone through a major change, you know. And this was your decision, remember?"

She snorts softly. "What a decision. Fall in line or kiss my ass goodbye."

That stings more than I'm going to admit. "And there I was thinking you chose out of love."

She immediately gives me a hard shove that surprises me, and I stumble backward. "We're not doing this, Luca!"

"You don't get to decide that."

"Yes, I sure as hell do," she fires back. "I'm leaving before we say something we both regret."

When she tries to slide past me along the desk's edge, I pin her in place again. "I'm not letting you out of my sight."

"Careful," she murmurs, looking me up and down. "You're sounding a lot more like a prison guard than a boyfriend."

I hate that she's right. I hate myself for saying that out loud. She has the power to bring out all the good in me, something I wasn't aware existed before I met her. She can also turn me into a raging fucking lunatic.

"I don't like the idea of you going off by yourself. Is that better?" I ask through clenched teeth, even forcing an empty smile.

"I understand, but I think it would be best if I went home, put on my PJs, and waited for you. We both need a minute to breathe. I'll go with Vinny if you want. As soon as I'm home, he can come back. God knows there are plenty of people around to keep an eye on me there." I hear the resentment behind that, and it chills my blood. She's unhappy. She's been trying hard to hide it, but every day that passes, she is a little more miserable.

Because of me.

Because I can't possibly give her what she needs.

"Yeah, you should go," I decide, and she gapes in surprise at my sudden change of heart, watching me cross the room and open the door to wave Vinny inside. "I want you to take her home," I tell him. "Straight home, straight back here. Understood?"

Vinny's eyes dart her way, quickly landing on me again. "Uh... sure. You okay?"

"I don't pay you for personal questions. Just keep her safe." Emilia is putting on her coat, and I help her without thinking, holding it while she slides her arms through the sleeves. It smells like her, and I catch a whiff of her perfume that threatens to melt the ice that has built itself around my heart.

Asshole, hold her. Apologize. You're fucking it all up.

Something won't let me do it—pride, most likely. I can identify, even if I can't do a thing about it any more than I can help loving her to the depths of my soul. I can't lose her, but I don't know how to give her what she needs. All I can do for now is follow them from the office down the narrow hall leading to the dance floor.

So this is what it means to love someone, to feel as helpless as I do now as I follow behind her while she follows Vinny. There's no way in hell I won't watch until she is safe in the car and Vinny pulls away. It's bad enough I have to send her off on her own.

I barely hear the high-pitched scream over the music from somewhere on the dance floor. Suddenly, everything moves in slow motion. I turn my head, seeking the source of the scream, and find a girl gaping in horror, her lips pulled back from her teeth as she raises her arm and points to a man standing only a few feet away from her.

A man who has raised a gun pointed in my direction.

In an instant, gunfire erupts, and I do the only thing instinct compels me to do. I throw myself over Emilia and take us both down while more screams pierce the air.

9

EMILIA

It all happened so fast. One second, I was following Vinny to the door with Luca behind me, and the next, I was hitting the floor, Luca's considerable weight pinning me. I went down hard enough to knock the air out of my lungs, and now I'm fighting the sick sensation of trying to take a breath but being unable to.

There are screams, so many screams, numerous feet running past. I'm afraid to move, or I might be trampled. Not that Luca would let me up, his arms crossed over the top of my head.

"Are you all right?" he shouts into my ear. Even so close, his voice barely rings out over the chaos that has erupted. I can only nod firmly to assure him while trying to wrap my head around what's happening.

Suddenly, the lights go up, and the music cuts off. "Everybody out!" a man shouts, though I get the feeling he doesn't need to. Everybody is already determined to get the hell out of here. I still don't entirely understand what's happening. Only a few moments have passed since I hit the floor, and it's all a blur. I think one of the bouncers is herding people out, and broken sobs and panicked shrieks fill the air before things start to quiet down.

Finally, Luca pushes himself up on his knees and helps me sit up. His hands run over my body, and for once, he's not looking to play around. "You're sure you weren't hurt? You weren't hit?" There's an edge to his voice, dark and primal.

Something deadly.

"No, really," I insist. The acrid odor of burnt powder fills the air, and adrenaline floods my system, but dammit, I feel alive. For the first time in weeks, I'm completely alive. I glance around, taking in the scene and assessing the damage as Luca helps me to my feet.

Nearly all the guests have fled by now, and the servers and bartenders are clustered behind the bar in a tight, wide-eyed group. "Go on home," Luca orders. "Everything will be fine here."

That leaves the bouncers to clean up the mess left behind that so many drunken partygoers dropped in favor of running for their lives. Nobody thought to stay and talk to the police. Maybe they figured it would be safer to get the hell out and pretend they weren't here.

I wonder what this will do to business.

"You okay, boss?" Vinny turns away from the body in the center of the sunken dance floor. "He didn't hit you, did he?"

"No, he was either a shitty shot, or my reflexes are quicker than he figured." Luca's arm snakes around my waist and pulls me close to him, and I'm glad for it. I need to be close to him now. If he had been only a second slower to realize what was happening, this could have gone much differently.

"You shot him?" I ask Vinny, who nods.

"Shame you couldn't have stopped at subduing him,"

Luca growls out. "I'd like to have had a word with the fucker."

I know what that means. I've seen it for myself back in the office. "We can assume who he was working for, though," I point out. "He probably has a record. Craig could look him up once you get an ID. You should call him directly and have him come down, take prints in case the guy isn't carrying an ID."

When all I get in return is silence, I look up to find Luca scowling. "Uh... yeah," he murmurs, stroking my cheek. "We'll do that. We have a procedure for when things like this happen." He might as well pat me on the head and offer me a cookie, but I get it. I might have been a cop, but this is the world he was raised in. He's probably been dealing with situations like this since I was in middle school.

"Of course. Force of habit," I offer with a shrug.

He runs a hand over my head, taking me by the back of the neck and pulling me close. "I wish I could kill that son of a bitch myself," he grits out through clenched teeth, closing his eyes and touching his forehead to mine as he takes one ragged breath after another. I feel his desperation, the hunger for vengeance fighting with hunger to be with me now. I know that feeling since I want nothing more than to be alone with him after such a close call. "Fuck, if I had lost you..."

"You didn't," I remind him. "I'm right here."

"Maybe you had better go now." He straightens, frowning but resolute. "Go home, wait for me like you were going to. I'll oversee the cleanup and make sure to handle things if anybody was stupid enough to call the cops. You can't be here if they show up. I'll be home as soon as I can."

"You're sure you're going to be all right?" I ask, something compelling me to cling tightly to him. Maybe it's because I understand how easily things could've gone much worse. He could've been hit. He was trying to protect me, but he could've taken a bullet. What would I do? What would I have then? He's everything to me. He's my whole world.

"I'll feel better knowing you're home, safe." It's the way he says it before kissing me that leads me to think this is my last night out for a long time. The only place he can really trust I'll be safe is within the compound's walls. I have to force myself into offering a reassuring smile as Luca orders Vinny to take me home.

Vinny goes out first to get the car, and one of the bouncers signals for me when he pulls up at the curb. Only once he's sure the coast is clear does Luca rush me out to the car and hurry me inside. I hate to think somebody could be watching and waiting, hoping to flush us out of the club for the real attack to begin. It doesn't seem to be that way, thank God, but what about next time? I won't pretend the possibility isn't there. I can't.

And now that I'm on my own in the back seat, I don't have to fight off the trembling when I consider how long this could go on.

IT'S CLOSING in on four in the morning when Luca steps into the house. I'm waiting for him on the couch, stretched out with my left leg propped up on a few pillows. He looks exhausted as he falls to his knees at my side. "What happened? You did get hurt, didn't you?" he asks, looking me over again, just as anxious as he was in the moments after the shots were fired.

"I'm just a little sore. I went down pretty hard, but it's

nothing a couple of ibuprofen couldn't handle." Now he's here, after hours of me staring at the television without paying attention to anything playing. How could I with my mind so far away? Looking at a bleak future without the man who is now holding me close, breathing hard, running his hands over me like he needs to remind himself I'm alive and well.

"Did the police show up?" I ask as he kisses my forehead.

Burying his face in my hair, he grunts. "No. I called Craig. He knows what to do to keep things quiet. He has procedures too."

I don't want to know about that. The sense of betrayal is still too strong. "Everything's okay now?"

"Everything is better than okay." His arms wrap around me and squeeze me tight. "It was torture not coming home with you. Not being with you when I think of fighting the way we did."

"I know," I whisper. I could only curse myself for wasting precious time bickering when I got home and changed, having nothing left to do but think. What if those had been our last moments together? I'd never forgive myself.

"I'm sorry. I'm so sorry." His lips are hot against my neck, my ear, and my cheek before finally finding my mouth. Something inside me rejoices, and I kiss him back as hard as I can, hard enough for my lips to sting. It doesn't stop me. I doubt anything could.

"I'm sorry," I gasp between kisses, running my hands through his hair, finally pushing his suit jacket away from his shoulders and over his arms. I have to touch him. I need the connection like I never have. "I should have been smarter about how I explained how I felt. I shouldn't have thrown it at you like I did, especially not at the club."

"No, no, don't do that." He pulls back, his hands buried in my hair to hold my head in place, and looks deep into my eyes. His love for me burning fiercely in those dark, swirling depths. The intensity of it is like a fire spreading from his body to mine. "I don't want you to ever feel like you need to be afraid to come to me with anything. I was selfish and stupid. I didn't know how to handle the way I felt. This is all new for me. I've never apologized to a woman before, for fuck's sake," he adds with a groan.

"I understand." And I do. It all seems so stupid now. Stupid and pointless. I kiss him again and again, pouring all of my love into it, whimpering, panting, and fumbling with the buttons on his shirt while he tugs at the waist of my yoga pants.

"Nothing matters more than you. Nothing." He slides a hand under my T-shirt and cups my breast, leaving me with no choice but to groan helplessly into his mouth and arch my back. My body is taking control, searching for what it needs, greedily accepting everything Luca can offer while demanding more. So much more.

At the end of the day, this is what matters—our connection. He's my purpose, my center, and only he can make my soul sing. He's my home.

He kisses his way over my body, almost rough, as he strips away my shirt so he can descend on me, claiming with his lips and tongue, with every touch of his knowing hands against my overheated skin. His touch is sweet fire, consuming me, stripping away everything but the basics. This, here and now. Us.

"Never fucking leave me," he rasps, his breath hot and moist on my stomach as he works his way up my body again, licking a trail between my breasts and up my throat.

"Not ever," I promise. But instead of pulling Luca closer

and drawing him inside me, I push him up and away from me with both hands. His confusion doesn't last long once I sit up, straddling his lap while he falls back against the cushions.

I strip his shirt away, running my hands over the intricately inked letters spanning his chest and lifting myself high enough to finish undoing his pants. He raises his hips and yanks them down along with his boxer briefs. Wrapping my fingers around his rigid length makes him suck in a sharp breath as he moans. "That's good. You make my cock feel so good."

"I know how to make it feel even better." I take a moment to savor the hold I have over him before taking him inside my aching pussy. After hours spent lost in helpless confusion, I need him deep inside me like a permanent reminder he's here with me, and that's all that matters.

Setting my own pace, I slowly slide down his length, watching sheer pleasure overtake him. He closes his eyes and lets his head fall back, groaning when I grind against his base. "Oh, fuck. That's it. Ride me," he grunts out, taking hold of my hips and squeezing until I suck in a pained breath. The brief flash of pain only intensifies the pleasure, making me drop down hard and fast, and we both moan when our bodies slam together.

He catches the back of my head with one hand, pulling me in for a deep, passionate kiss that steals my breath. I move my tongue in time with the slow, rhythmic grinding of my hips, drinking in every deep, guttural moan that comes from the man now inside me. When I pull back, gasping for air, he runs his lips over my throat, planting kisses against my collarbone, worshiping my breasts while I rock my hips harder and faster, swept up in that special potent magic that only comes to life between us.

"Fuck, so good," Luca grits out through his clenched jaw, overcome as I am, jerking upward with his hips to match my strokes. He wraps my hair around his fist and pulls my head back possessively, making me wince but making me ride harder. Something about it gets my heart racing faster. "You're mine. Say it," he demands.

"Yours," I whimper out, grinding desperately. "I'm yours." He captures my mouth again, invading me, and I drink him in.

Sweet Lord, it's so good. The pressure against my clit is almost unbearable, and the friction between our bodies has me ready to burst into flames. The tension rises as I chase my release, holding him tight and running my nails over his skin while he grunts against my neck.

So close. I just need a little bit more.

"Come for me," he growls out, and the words have their intended effect. My orgasm takes over so intensely I clutch him close, needing to hold him as I ride it out, my hips still jerking. Jolts of aftershocks pulse through me, my body tensing, and my breath chokes me.

Luca groans, his release hitting him with force. He grabs my hips, holding me in place as he bucks up into me, sending a rush of warmth deep inside. With a final jerk, a growl reverberates deep in his chest, and I fall against him, weak now, exhausted but exhilarated.

His heart races against mine but begins to slow down as we stay locked together in a tight embrace. No one is going to pull us apart.

Not now, not ever.

Because while I belong to him, he belongs to me.

10

LUCA

"That's fine. We'll be there soon. I'm expecting everything to be in order when we arrive." With that, I end the call, lifting a hand to let Vinny know we'll be on our way shortly. He's leaning against the limousine in a holding pattern.

Opening the door, I step into the house, and even though the door to the bedroom is closed, the scent of Emilia's perfume hangs in the air. A smile stirs my lips, and I clear my throat, raising my voice. "How's it going? Do we have an estimate of how much longer until we can leave?"

"Sorry!" she calls back through the closed door. "I'm sorry, just a few more minutes. I want to look my best."

"You looked your best when you woke up this morning," I call back, checking the time on my Rolex. Not that it matters. It isn't like we have a reservation dictating our schedule. But she doesn't know that.

We need this. She deserves a night out, and as for me, I need a diversion. There's guilt, of course. My father is up there in the house, and for all I know, he could be dying. Fuck knows I'll never get a straight answer out of anybody.

It seems even Dante has clued into the fact there's something we are not being told. I've noticed him watching Papa when he isn't looking. His narrow-eyed expression and the tight set of his jaw scream out his concern.

Would he come to me about it, though? Ask for my thoughts on whether we should try to convince the man to see a doctor if he hasn't already? Of course not. My opinion means shit.

This can't go on forever. I can create all the diversions, but that won't change anything. I can't help feeling like I'm running away from my troubles as I look forward to a night with the woman I love, but then life can't be put on permanent hold, either. As she made very clear a few nights ago in my office, she already feels like she's sacrificed enough. I can't ask her to put her needs aside indefinitely.

My heart stutters at the click of the doorknob, signaling she's coming out. I turn, eager to see the results of Emilia's hours of preparation.

How can I have indulged in every inch of this woman's body, yet she still has the power to take my breath away? I am completely helpless at the sight of her. Loose waves of hair frame her face and cascade over her shoulders. Her eyes burn with a love so fierce it mirrors my own and draws the breath from my lungs.

The silver dress gleams and sparkles with every move she makes, the fabric sliding over her curves like water. This must be another dress she picked up during her trip with Guilia, and the effect is enough that I'd happily encourage her to make their shopping trips a regular thing because, holy shit, all I want is to pin her to the bed and fuck her until I can't see straight.

Her brow lifts at the shuddering breath I release.

Instantly, she looks down at herself. "Is it not right? You didn't give me a dress code. I can change."

"I say this with love," I rasp, shaking my head. "I would break your arms before I let you change out of that dress."

Her cheeks go red. "I guess you approve."

"If I weren't half starved, I would show you here and now how much I approve. You are so beautiful, so damn sexy, it's unfair. How am I supposed to do anything but stare at you?" I hold out my hands, and she comes to me, still blushing, but she can't hide a satisfied grin.

The silver stilettos encasing her feet mean I don't have to lean down quite as far to kiss her, sweeping my tongue along the seam of her lips, stroking hers with it. She purrs, and the sound goes straight to my cock.

I suspect I have a very uncomfortable night ahead. But it's the sweetest torture, the sort I would happily suffer endlessly.

"So?" she asks, brightening up now that I've left no question about how incredible she looks. "Do I get to know where we're going?"

I pretend to think it over, shaking my head. "Don't worry. You'll know soon enough. Have a little patience." It's too much fun messing with her. It always has been. Watching her frustrated little frown furrow her brow stretches my smile into my cheeks.

"So long as I'm not overdressed." She accepts my help getting into her coat, and I take a moment to lean in and inhale her perfume. I'll never be able to smell its fresh, sweet scent after tonight without thinking of this moment. How exquisite she looks. How deeply in love with her I am. I can't remember a time when I wasn't. She's that much a part of me.

Her soft gasp upon stepping out of the house and

finding the waiting limousine lights me up inside. It makes everything worth it. "Wow! A limo too? I feel like a princess in a fairy tale."

"I told you, I want this to be a special night for us." Yet, as I take her hand to lead her to where Vinny has now opened the door, I notice her hesitation, the way she stumbles a little, taking a step.

"What's wrong?" I ask, turning to her, forgetting the limo for a minute to address whatever has creased her brow.

"I'm being silly." When I continue to stare at her, waiting, she sighs. "Is it safe? I'm sorry. I don't want to sound ungrateful, and I'm not trying to ruin anything, but after what happened..."

"You're afraid to be out in public with me," I conclude with a sinking heart, which I try like hell to conceal.

Her eyes pop open wide. "No! Shit, that's not what I meant. I'm worried about *you*, Luca. I don't want you to take any unnecessary risks for my sake. I'm the one who made a big deal about never going out anywhere, and now?" There's pain in her voice, and it's written across her perfect face.

"Enough." Taking both of her hands in mine, I murmur, "If I thought there was any risk, we wouldn't go anywhere. I would never willingly put you in harm's way. I've also taken precautions tonight. Believe me, we have nothing to worry about."

She seems happier and more confident as we continue walking to the car, and by the time she slides inside, she's smiling again.

I can't keep my hands off her during the ride, touching her legs, teasing us both.

"You look good enough that I'm ready to go straight to dessert so we can get out of there quicker," I growl out while indulging in her silky skin.

She leans toward me, giving me a nice view of her luscious tits. If she leans any farther, they'll come spilling out, and fuck, do I wish they would. The privacy divider is up, meaning no one would see but me. "We can always get our food to go," she offers seductively.

"Damn, woman. You have no idea how good that sounds right now." Or maybe she does, closing her eyes and sighing when I run the back of my fingers over the swells of her tits. She's not wearing a bra, meaning her nipples stand out against the flowing fabric, drawing my hungry gaze.

Then I remember the trouble I went through putting the night together, and it's just enough to temper the erection raging in my pants. "Later," I promise in a whisper, groaning when she bites her lip.

When she realizes we're driving into Brooklyn, she smiles at me. "Where are you taking me?"

"For an excellent meal." Much of the weight that's sat so heavy on my chest lately lightens thanks to the delight in her smile. I can let myself release some of my worries for her sake. She deserves that much for a few hours.

I watch as she chews her lip, craning her neck to see out the windows before we finally pull to a stop in front of a charming little restaurant in Williamsburg. Her jaw damn near hits her lap. "No way. You need to make reservations like a month in advance to get in here," she gasps, her eyes widening in surprise.

"Six months. Anyway, I pulled some strings." A lot of strings. Very expensive ones. But I made it work, and while I knew it would be worth it, I would now gladly do this again a hundred times over if it meant witnessing the joy that erupted from her. "But that's not all," I add.

She's beside herself, throwing her hands into the air.

"What else could there be? I've been dying to eat here since I first moved to Brooklyn."

"Come with me." Vinny opens the door, and I step out into the clear, cold evening, extending a hand for her to follow.

She wears a hesitant expression but follows me, and I notice her frown when she identifies the obvious. "It looks closed. Are they closed?"

"For everyone but us." Opening the door to the restaurant, it's dark except for candles set up on every table, along with lush bouquets of crimson red roses, which fill the dining room with their fragrance. I'm not what anyone would call a romantic, but I can admit to myself the effect is striking.

Her gasp confirms this. "It's incredible. Do you mean to tell me you booked the entire restaurant for us?" she whispers in awe as her lashes flutter over her wide, shining eyes.

"I wanted it to be just the two of us."

"Luca, It's like something out of a dream." She lowers her head and breathes deeply as we pass one of the tables, almost burying her nose in the blooms and smiling. "They're so beautiful."

Her enjoyment only sweetens my next announcement. "I'm having them all brought home for us when we're finished here."

"Our home is about to become a botanical bonanza." She's like a little kid, overflowing with joy, and I could get addicted to seeing her like this. I plan to make it my life's mission to put that look on her face time and time again.

"I can't believe you went to all this trouble for me," she whispers, and her chin trembles a little when we reach the only table in the restaurant currently set for dinner with napkins and silverware.

"Hey." I run a hand over her shining hair, tenderly cupping the back of her neck and drawing her close. "This is nothing. I would do anything for you. You're my woman, Emilia. You deserve the fucking world."

Her eyes soften under my gaze. "I already have it," she reminds me, tipping her head back to accept my kiss.

Someone clears their throat in the back of the room, and Emilia breaks our kiss. I grunt out my disappointment as we take the hint to sit and get ready to eat.

After a brief chat with the chef, we're treated to a vintage bottle of wine, then a multi-course tasting menu featuring the homemade pasta the restaurant is best known for. As we eat, we talk like two people on a date, letting the conversation wander. She tells me about the one and only time she tried to make pasta from scratch, and I tell her about the one and only time I tried to cook it for me, Dante, Niccolo, and Frankie, whose name still stirs heat in my chest. It's a story that's always made me laugh, but his memory tinges it somewhat.

"Listen, I had no idea how much a pound of pasta actually is," I explain while sopping up the peppery cream sauce with a crust of bread. "I figured I usually put it away by the truckful, and so did the guys. So here I am, staring down a pantry full of boxed noodles, and I thought a pound apiece should do the trick."

"A pound each?" Emilia sets down her fork, covering her mouth with one hand as she hoots with laughter.

"There I was, thinking there was nothing to it... figuring I could take care of things while my parents were out." The memory makes me laugh even as I cringe at the mess I made. "Mama laughed it off after she finished chasing me around, screaming in Italian."

"I bet you were adorable when you were little." Her eyes

twinkle in the candlelight when they meet mine from across the small table.

"I was a pain in the ass," I tell her with a shrug. "I can accept it. Dante was older, and I always wanted to strut around and prove I was tough shit too."

"But I bet you had a heart of gold."

I don't have the heart to tell her that sort of thing doesn't get you far in our world. Then again, I'm sure she knows. She's familiar enough, thanks to the work she used to do.

"You know, it didn't hit me until just now," I realize, and Emilia arches an eyebrow, silently questioning my meaning. "You never talk about your family. I know your parents exist, but you never bring them up."

She swallows a mouthful of tender ravioli, then dabs the corners of her mouth with a napkin. "There's not much to tell. I don't have brothers and sisters and cousins like you do. I'm the only child of two people who live on the other side of the country from their siblings," she explains.

"I'm looking forward to meeting your parents when they return from their trip."

That's not exactly the truth. There are roughly a hundred other things on my to-do list that take precedence. But I'm sure having us all together would make her happy.

Then why does she look troubled, like I suggested we strip naked before enjoying dessert? "I'm sure we'll work something out. So long as you think it's safe," she adds in a voice devoid of the energy it held moments ago.

Of course. I should've thought of that. "I would never put them in harm's way. We'll play it by ear," I vow, and now her smile seems sincere again. I hate to think she's worried about what my presence in her life means to her safety, but it's a fact that can't be avoided. It would be childish of me to try.

By the time I help her into the limo, we're both full and happy. I want to hold onto this feeling, to put it in a box and carry it in my pocket. Sadly, life doesn't work that way. I'm learning we can only try to be grateful for these moments when they happen. God knows I've seen my share of misery and pain.

So has Emilia, though none of it shows in her almost drowsy smile as she practically drapes herself over me as we pull away from the restaurant and the privacy divider is up again.

"You know," she whispers in my ear while her leg slides over mine. "I'm going to have to find a way to pay you back for all the trouble you went to."

Hello. My dick likes the sound of that, stirring to life in an instant. "What did you have in mind?" I murmur, resting my hand on her thigh and slowly easing the silver fabric higher.

"I have a few ideas." The heat of her breath fans over my skin as she places a lingering kiss against my cheek, turning my head and stroking my mouth open with her tongue.

It's enough to sit here and drive each other crazy, going slowly, making out like a couple of teenagers. Feeling her up while she strokes my throbbing erection through my pants, teasing each other with one deep, slow kiss after another.

My nerves sizzle by the time she breaks away and begins lowering my zipper. "Emilia?" I murmur, sliding down a little in the seat, spreading my thighs wider while she gets on her knees in front of me. Our eyes connect for the briefest moment, and a wave of lust sweeps over me when I recognize the wickedness flickering in those blue depths.

"Just relax, Mr. Santoro," she whispers, and the sensual tone of her voice leaves me closing my eyes while she frees me from my prison and runs her tongue around the ridge of my swollen head.

"Fuck, yeah, just like that..." I reach for her, stroking her hair while she continues driving me out of my mind, going slowly, leaving me holding my breath as I wait for the next lick. It's like I'm walking a tightrope, completely focused on what she's doing, afraid to make a move that might shatter the moment.

A groan of pure relief stirs in my chest when she parts her lips and takes me inside, sinking inch by inch until I tap the back of her throat. She still hasn't taken all of me, so she wraps a hand around my base to make up for it, moving it in time with her slow, sensual strokes.

I'm on fire, burning from the inside out, running my hands through her hair and moving my hips in time with her bobbing head. Fuck, if only this could last forever, with nothing in the world mattering but the soft moans coming from the woman sucking my cock like it's the last thing she'll ever do, and her fucking life depends on it.

"So good." I moan, fighting to hold on but knowing it's a losing battle. When she runs her tongue along the under-side, pressing it firmly, flicking it across the bundle of nerves under my head, fireworks explode in my skull. "Oh, fuck, you're so good. You're gonna make me come. Is that what you want? You want to make me come?"

"Mm-hmm..." The pressure from her tongue intensifies as she hollows out her cheeks, sucking harder, bobbing faster.

"You want me to come in your mouth? So you can swallow every drop?"

She answers with a long, high-pitched moan that adds to the unbearable sensations, making me jerk my hips faster, holding her head still until I'm fucking her mouth, racing to the edge, focused on nothing more than coming down her throat. And when I do, it's intense enough to make my ears ring and my hands shake. I'm dizzy by the time I finish, and she lifts her head after swallowing my seed. "Holy shit," I breathe out, then laugh at myself while she takes her place beside me again. "If I had known that was coming, I would've bought out a restaurant way before now."

She only snuggles up next to me with a happy little sigh. "I figured it was the least I could do. And it's not like I don't get anything out of it." When I frown because I can't imagine what she means, she grins. "Believe me. You could drown in my panties right now."

"That sounds like a challenge to me," I growl out, but she only laughs and swats my hand away when I try to test her statement.

"Later. That was just for you." Now, she's content to rest her head on my shoulder, and I'm more than happy to have her there. If anything, she's giving me time to entertain an idea that's been bubbling in the back of my mind for a while.

It's not enough for us to share a single night like this. She deserves more.

And I might be able to enlist my mother's help.

I could soon have another surprise up my sleeve if all goes well.

11

EMILIA

I must still be sleeping.

Dreaming about having the hottest man I've ever met between my legs, licking me and chafing my inner thighs with the scruff on his cheeks, grunting softly as he eats me with abandon.

No dream could be this good.

"Yes, just like that." I lift my hips to grind against his face, groaning when he does.

What a way to wake up. He couldn't wait to go down on me. *This man is so hungry for me.* The thought alone tightens my core and makes me whimper while he traces circles over my clit with his tongue.

"Shit! Don't stop." I gather the sheets in my fists, twisting and tugging while my head rolls from side to side. It's so much all at once, too much to take, but I would die if he stopped and left me hanging so close to the edge.

He chuckles at my high-pitched whine when he slides two of his thick fingers inside me, stroking my inner walls, teasing my G-spot while his tongue strokes my clit. I can't take it. It's too much, yet somehow it's just enough. "Yes! Oh

God, yes!" My legs clench around his head as I ride it out, bucking and gasping until a warm, sweet sense of peace washes over me. My muscles go limp, and I sink back against the mattress, my legs falling to the sides.

He takes his time kissing his way along the insides of my thighs before rolling away. I open my eyes in time to catch the shit-eating grin he wears like he's proud of his performance. "What about you?" I manage to croak, eyeing his very obvious erection as it sways with every step he takes away from the bed.

"That was for you," he assures me, entering the bathroom. "I have back-to-back meetings up at the house. If I'm late, it's your fault for looking so hot while you're sleeping." He closes the door, and the shower turns on a moment later. I curl into a happy ball and pull a sheet over my naked body, still basking in the afterglow of an intense orgasm.

It feels like only a few seconds pass, but when I open my eyes again, Luca is tying a knot in a silk necktie, standing in front of the full-length mirror on the back of the bedroom door. Apparently, I must have drifted back off. "You're not having meetings with any women, are you?" I ask, propping my head on my hand and drinking in the sight of him wearing a charcoal gray suit and crisp white shirt.

"Uh... no. Why would I?" he asks, smirking at my reflection before turning to me.

"I don't want some random woman falling for you, looking like you do." I make sure to growl a little the way he always does when feeling jealous or possessive, which is pretty much most of the time.

"It doesn't matter what unfortunate woman falls for me. They might as well not exist." He strolls my way and leans down for a kiss, smiling down at me. "I'm taken. There isn't another pussy in existence that could possibly compare to yours," he announces, backing away again.

"I'll take that as a compliment," I murmur, narrowing my eyes.

"That's how I meant it. Oh, and do me a favor." He offers a sexy smirk as he turns to me, framed in the doorway. "Stay this way. I'm going to want more of that world-class pussy when I come back later."

"Stay like this, you mean?" I stretch my arms over my head until the sheet falls away from my body. His growl makes me giggle, though it also sparks fresh heat between my legs. I cannot get enough of him.

"You're a menace." He takes one last look, then turns away with a miserable groan, and I laugh to myself again when I hear him grumbling as he leaves the house.

As lovely an idea as it is, lying in bed all day and waiting for him to come back and ravish me is not very practical. I get up, quickly strip the bed, then toss the sheets into the wash before heading for the shower. It's easy to sing my heart out on a morning like this, and I do. I sing until the entire bathroom is full of steam and the water starts to run a little cooler.

I feel like a new woman when I emerge, freshly scrubbed and blissfully happy. The date with Luca and the few days that have passed since then have been like a dream. It helps that the house is chock full of luscious roses, reminding me of that night and all the pains Luca took to make me happy. That alone is enough to touch me deeply and make me smile fondly as I go through the motions of drying my hair and getting dressed.

My good mood lasts until I grab my phone from the nightstand, where it's been sitting face down since I left it there last night. Everything comes crashing down at the sight of a missed call from Mom.

Her timing is nothing if not impeccable. Now I'm like a deflated balloon, dragging my feet out to the kitchen to make coffee. She left a voicemail, too, but I don't think I'm strong enough to listen to it yet. I need a little caffeine first.

Maybe a lot.

There's only so long I can put off the inevitable. Fixing myself a cup, I sit at the counter and offer a silent prayer to whoever might be listening as I pull up the voicemail, touching the play button.

"Emilia Jane, enough is enough." She launched right into it, didn't she? Why waste time? "I am going to have to go down to the station and start raising a little hell if I don't get some answers from you. Where are you? Why have you not been home yet? Why are your things still missing? What sort of job do they have you on that requires you to move half of the things out of your apartment? I'm going to ask questions, and I'm not going to stop until I get answers. So either you call me back and tell me what I want to know, or I speak to your supervisor. Make your choice."

As if there is one.

My hands shake hard enough to make gripping the phone a challenge. I call her back right away, hoping like hell she hasn't gone ahead with whatever cockeyed scheme she has in mind. For once, I need her to be rational. I should've known that was too much to ask.

"There you are," she practically shouts, answering on the first ring. "So that's what it took? Threatening to go over your head and talk to your boss?" Her shrill voice leaves me wincing. I think I'm getting a headache.

"Could you please not yell at me like I'm the enemy?" I demand, forcing myself to take a deep breath before I lose it.

"Could you please not go out of your way to avoid my calls and messages? What am I supposed to think? You could've been dead for all I knew. Why have you not gone home?"

"Here's a question for you," I counter. I sound much too angry—because I am—but there are certain things I can't pretend to be okay with. "Why do you keep going to my apartment? I was not even aware you still had the spare key, much less that you come and go as you please."

"Is it wrong for me to want to keep you safe and healthy?" she asks in that saintly voice that always makes me want to shriek until I lose my voice.

"So you break into my apartment?"

"I'm using your spare key," she reminds me. "I would hardly call that breaking in."

"You are there without my permission or even my knowledge, Mom."

"Since when do I need permission to check in on my child?" she asks, and the worst part is, I think she believes herself.

"Since I signed the lease, Mom. I'm an adult. You can't go in and out of my home without me knowing about it." God forbid somebody from the Vitali crew is watching. A sickening chill washes over me and leaves me fighting back nausea. "Please, promise me you will not do that again. It's important."

"More secrecy?" she asks. "More mysteries?"

Help me with this woman. "Mom, I'm serious. It's part of my job. I *am* a detective. Don't do it again. Please," I beg, and I'm not above sounding scared because, well, I am.

She keeps me waiting a second before breaking her silence. "You are starting to frighten me, Emilia." There's no more shrill demand. She's somber, which is somehow worse. "This isn't you. You aren't secretive. You don't disappear for weeks at a time. We used to talk almost every day. What's changed?"

Everything. Absolutely every aspect of my life has changed in the months since I wished my parents good luck as they left on their trip. I'm a different person now. And there is no way for me to explain it to her. I wouldn't know where to begin.

"Please, Mom," I murmur. "Listen to me. It's important. I can tell you everything, but not just yet. Soon, I swear, but not yet. I need you to trust me. And I need you to respect my privacy more than anything. That's the most important part of all. Can you do that for me?" I hope she hears the trembling in my voice and takes it seriously.

"Emilia..."

What's it going to take? Do I have to threaten to call the cops on her for breaking in? "Please, Mom."

"All right, fine. You can have your precious privacy. But I don't know how much longer I can take this... me, or your father, who is just as worried about you, if not more so. Do you want to do this? If you don't care about me, do you at least care about him?" I have to give it to her. She has the ability to pivot on a dime and attack from another direction.

"You know I love you both." I am much too old for her to guilt me like this, but that's another issue. I have more than enough to deal with as it is. "I need to go. I love you. Please, trust me."

It's clear by the time I set the phone down that I need to either piss or get off the pot—one of my dad's favorite sayings. They need to know, and I need to figure out how to tell them.

No matter how sure I am, they will never understand.

"I THOUGHT I would make us a nice dinner." I step back from the table, and though my heart is racing with dread, it's nice to see Luca looking so pleased as he loosens his tie.

"How did you know this is exactly what I needed to come home to?" He looks at me with so much love and appreciation while all I can do is wrestle with guilt. I've been fighting myself all day, wondering how the hell I'm supposed to balance my old life and my new life. Blaming myself for putting it off until now.

"It's not exactly Michelin quality, but I do make a good meatball," I assure him as he takes his seat and starts dishing out food while telling me about his meetings today.

"Apparently, Alessandro knows which families have aligned with us, and he's decided to fuck with them. Low-level shit, nuisances, but it'll only get worse." He's scowling as he drapes a napkin over his lap, a scowl that only deepens when he looks my way. "You don't need to hear about this. There's a reason we never discuss business at the dinner table."

"If there is something on your mind that's bothering you, I want to hear about it. I'm here for you," I remind him.

"I know," he says with a brief smile. "This is for me to worry about, not you. It isn't fair."

Picking up my silverware, I shrug. "Well, whatever you think is best."

His head snaps back a little, and his chewing slows. "What?" he mumbles around a mouthful of food.

"What?" I blink rapidly, shrugging. "What did I say?"

"Whatever I think is best? Since when?" He's chuckling, so I know he's not offended or anything. I also know I made a mistake. I have to relax.

"I'm just saying. I'm not trying to push you into opening up. You can take the lead when it comes to stuff like this."

"How generous of you." There's something about the way he lifts an eyebrow that leads me to think he's suspicious. "How was your day?"

"Fine."

His eyebrow lifts higher as he looks around. "You've used so much lemon-scented cleaner today. It's all I can smell. What's up? What has you so anxious?"

Am I that obvious? I suppose a sparkling house, a home-cooked dinner, and the fact that I have only been able to play with my food rather than eat any adds up to trouble. "Now that you mention it, there is something I wanted to talk about." I can't put it off any longer.

"I knew it." Still, he keeps eating. "This is delicious, by the way. Don't tell Mama, but I prefer your meatballs to hers."

"I would never dream of insulting her that way." We share a soft laugh, and I'm glad because it eases a fraction of the nerves that have gripped me all day. "I might as well come right out and say it. My parents came home earlier than expected, and they've been bugging me to see them."

His features draw together in an expression of concern. "Why didn't you mention this earlier? Did it just happen today?"

"No, not exactly," I hedge, and now my heart is beating faster.

He arches an eyebrow. "Exactly when did they return?"

"Last week, maybe late the week before? I don't quite remember."

Setting down his silverware, he wipes his mouth, staring at me the whole time. Tossing his napkin onto the table, he asks, "And you didn't think it was worth telling me?"

My attempt at laughter falls flat. "I didn't think you would take it that seriously," I murmur with my heart in my throat.

His lowered brow and the hardening of his gaze do not bode well. "I've never met your parents. As far as I've known, they've been out of the country all this time. Now you're telling me they're back. How did they react to your resignation?"

This is all wrong. I should've approached it differently. Now he's asking questions I can't answer and staring at me until I have to look down at my plate to avoid his gaze. "I didn't tell her. Let me explain," I add in a louder voice when he throws his hands into the air and mutters angrily in Italian. "That's not the kind of news you just drop on somebody during a phone conversation."

"What were you planning to do? Take out an ad in the paper?" he jeers, smirking.

"I wanted to talk with you about it before I said anything in case I need to be careful."

"But you didn't talk to me about it," he points out through clenched teeth. "You kept it a secret. Have you been afraid to talk to me?"

I can't help but scoff, though that is part of it. "Face it, you already have more than enough on your plate. This is my problem, and I have to come up with a solution."

"We're together now, so there's no such thing as your problems or my problems. They're *our* problems."

"Says the guy who doesn't want to talk about work over dinner," I remind him, snorting.

His nostrils flare with every breath, each a little shakier than the last. "That's different, and you know it. Tell me the truth. Why are you so hesitant to tell your parents you left your job and we're together?"

"Why do you think?" I can't help laughing, though, not because anything is funny. I don't understand him. "Luca, come on. I love you, I want to be with you, but let's not pretend there isn't anything complicated about our relationship."

"You don't have to tell me that," he murmurs, and I know he's thinking about everything he's gone through for us.

"The second I announce your name, they're going to know who I'm talking about, and it's going to shock them. Same thing with the job. They don't know I was shot. They don't know I was taken. They don't know we've ever met, much less that we're in a relationship and I'm living on your father's estate. And once they find out all of this, they're going to lose their minds." I wish I were exaggerating. If anything, I'm underplaying it. "Do you see how complicated this is?"

"All I see is two people in love who want to make a life together. Career changes happen all the time." He even shrugs, like any of this is that simple.

"You don't know my parents," I remind him with a dry laugh.

"Because you won't let me," he counters.

"For fuck's sake, it's not that simple! Just like it wasn't simple for you." Touching a hand to my chest, I explain, "I can make the choice for myself to be here, to be with you because I can weigh the dangers. I know what I'm dealing with, and I can make an informed decision. They can't. Vitali or anybody else gets wind of me having parents living nearby... what do you think is going to happen? I have to think of them, too, just like you have to think about your family."

He holds up a finger. "There's a difference. Only one of us is willing to risk everything."

"What have I not risked? My life, my job, my reputation. And at least your family can defend themselves. My parents? A lawyer and a retired school teacher? What the hell are they supposed to do?"

"I'll put a detail on them!" he shouts, infuriating me when he rolls his eyes.

"Oh, and I'm sure none of the neighbors will think anything weird about that. Think, Luca. You've never been part of the actual, real world. This is much more complicated than you're making it out to be." I hate making him flinch at my accusation, but it's the truth. He only thinks he knows what's at stake.

A wide range of emotions pass over his face, his features hardening into a cold mask I witnessed back in the early days of our acquaintance. "I guess there's only one answer, then. I guess this is all too much, and I was out of my fucking mind to think otherwise."

"Don't do this," I beg when he gets up from the table.

He responds by shoving his chair back violently, sweeping an arm over his side of the table, and knocking his plate to the floor. Red sauce splatters over the freshly washed hardwood, but the way he is glaring at me chills my blood.

"I'm good enough for you to fuck," he growls out, taking one slow step after another around the table to where I wait, frozen in fear. "I'm good enough for you to play house with. But you never had any intention of this being forever."

"That's not true." I whimper while he leans down, a hand on either arm of my chair. There's no choice but to lean away, though there's no escaping his growing rage. "I love you. I want to be with you."

"So long as the rest of the world doesn't know, so you don't have to be embarrassed," he concludes.

Seeing the blank fury in his eyes is breaking my heart, where I'm used to seeing nothing but love. I have to believe it's still in there, that we can get through this. "That's not true," I insist weakly. "You want to protect the people who matter to you. I feel the same way about my family."

I'm face-to-face with a wild animal. Unpredictable. What's he going to do? Throw me out? Maybe something worse? He bares his teeth, snarling like he wants nothing more than to break me, and I flinch but won't look away. My reaction makes him shove away from the chair with a growl. "Don't bother waiting up for me tonight," he grits out, turning his back. He doesn't look my way as he leaves, his footsteps ringing out like an accusation. "I'll sleep up at the house."

I could plead with him to stay so we can talk things out, but I'm angry too. This whole situation is so fucked up.

He pauses with his hand on the doorknob, his shoulders rising and falling with every ragged breath. "I can't be here right now. You want me to go. Trust me." With that, he flings the door open, then slams it closed on his way out.

I don't know how much time passes, but I can't do anything except sit and stare at the mess on the floor until tears blur my vision. What are we going to do? How are we going to make this work?

And can I really put everyone I love at risk?

12

LUCA

A meat sandwich eaten at one in the morning in an otherwise silent kitchen is a far cry from the feast Emilia prepared. However, after hours spent working on the correspondence Papa has been too "tired" to handle recently, my empty stomach would no longer be ignored.

Something about sitting on my own in darkness, pierced only by the light over the stove, is profoundly depressing. I hear every creak in the old house and every breath I take. There's nothing to mute the accusations in my head.

I fucked it all up. I let myself become so furious, wanting to hurt the woman I love so she'd understand what I was suffering. Once the rage faded, there was nothing but shame left behind. I'm supposed to be better than this. I need to be better. I don't know how, and I doubt a night spent in my old bedroom will help me work it out.

Soft footfalls fill the air as I finish eating. My chest throbs for one breathless second before I remind myself Emilia wouldn't come up here. Another second passes, then my mother appears, jumping with a gasp at the sight of me sitting at the island across from the stove. "*Merda!*" she breathes, clasping her hands over her chest. "You scared me to death!"

"I thought you were in bed, asleep. What are you doing up so late?"

"I was not aware I reached the age where I need permission to be up past midnight." Her lips twitch with humor while she crosses the kitchen in a flowing pink robe that billows behind her like a sail. She reaches the stove and picks up the kettle, shaking it around to see if there's any water inside. "Besides, I could ask you the same question."

Rather than let her see me wince, I stare down at what's left of my sandwich. "I have a lot on my mind," I mutter.

"Shouldn't you be with Emilia? Telling her about it so you can work it out together?" Filling the kettle, she sets it on the burner. "Or is she what's on your mind?"

She stands opposite me and folds her arms on the island counter, smirking. "What did you do?"

"What makes you assume I did anything?" I'm sure my defensiveness isn't going to help.

The humor fades from her eyes, the smile from her lips. "Because that's how this goes, my boy. I love you, but at the end of the day, you are still a man. And men aren't known for being able to keep from making asses out of themselves."

That's hardly the saltiest language I've ever heard, but from her? I have to laugh in disbelief. "Please, tell me how you really feel," I offer, spreading my arms to the sides. "Let me have it."

I wasn't serious, but she takes it that way. "I will. You are a headstrong, impatient, sometimes infuriating young man." Tipping her head to the side, she sighs. "And from what I can tell, you've met your match." At least she manages to sound sympathetic.

"I need time to myself to breathe and figure things out," I tell her.

"Like what? Whether or not you love the girl?" she gently prompts.

"I know that already." It's the only thing I'm sure of.

"Then what else is there?"

"She's been lying to me. Pretending she told her family about us, about resigning, all of it. She's ashamed of me," I confess. Fuck, the words lodge in my throat and threaten to choke me. My mother is the only person on the planet with whom I would speak this freely, yet I can barely get through it.

Her brows knit together in a familiar expression of concern. "So she told you she spoke with them, but she didn't?"

"Not exactly," I admit, already seeing her point and hating it.

"You assumed?" she prompts, gentle but firm.

"It was a lie of omission," I counter.

"Maybe she guessed how you would react? Just as she knows how her family will react? Luca," she murmurs, mournfully shaking her head. "Above all things, we must be honest with ourselves. We aren't a normal family. They're civilians, average people. We are not, and because she's associated with us, she must live here. She'll be safe while things flare up with our enemies. They don't have that luxury. Even if we were in peacetime now, your relationship would be a lot for those people to swallow. Have some compassion. She only wants everyone to be happy."

Why does it sound so fucking simple when she puts it that way? Why do I want to kick myself in the ass for being a stubborn prick?

Still, it doesn't solve everything. "What does this mean

for the future? What if they refuse to accept her choice, and she ends up spending the rest of her life questioning her decision to be with me? How do I live with that possibility?"

"You take a leap of faith and trust things are going to work out. It's all you can do." When I sit back with a groan, she asks, "You're sure you love the girl?"

"I love her so much that I hate her for it sometimes."

I'm ashamed of myself for saying it, but all she does is offer a knowing smile. "Yes, that sounds about right. Only the people you love the most can make you feel that way."

"What do I do? How do I make this work with everything stacked against us?"

"If it's real, you will find a way," she assures me.

"That's not good enough," I insist.

"You'll figure it out together because she loves you too." I can't believe she would laugh at a time like this, but she does, shaking her head. "There's nothing like a fight in the beginning when you first get together. It feels like the end of the world, but you get over it."

"This isn't some childish argument," I mutter.

"So why are you sulking here like a child?" she asks.

I doubt Emilia could say something like that without my temper flaring. Mama might be the only one who can, and even then, it's not easy to keep myself in check at the insult. "I was afraid of what might happen if I didn't leave."

Her lips draw together in a disapproving frown, but she still nods. "Sometimes it is best to walk away and cool off. But you aren't solving anything by hanging around here. That girl is down there all alone, probably crying her heart out because she's stuck between what she wants and what she knows the consequences are going to be. That's not your fault. She chose you. She had to know there would be challenges. But, son, you're not helping by becoming angry.

You're only adding to the problem." She reaches across the counter to squeeze my hand, then turns away at the whistling kettle.

I mull it over while she fixes a cup of tea. How am I supposed to help Emilia through this when it's obvious she sees me as part of the problem? "I can't lose her," I grunt out.

"The only way you could lose her is if you let your pride get in the way again." She gives me a stern gaze over her shoulder. "It hurt your pride to think she might hesitate to introduce her family to the one she's part of now. You want everything to be easy for her. You don't want her to ever regret choosing you."

"That's true," I admit, as much as I hate to.

"Try to keep that in mind the next time there's an argument brewing. There's nothing wrong with being disappointed, but taking it out on her is unacceptable. I raised you better than that." She pats my shoulder in passing, and for a moment, I wish life was as simple as back in the day when a pat on the shoulder or a tight hug fixed things. "You're better than that. I know you are."

I have my doubts. "I want to be better for *her*."

She passes again in the other direction, only this time, she gives me a gentle shove. "For heaven's sake, Luca, support her."

I must be the world's biggest ass. Everything Mom says makes sense. I needed to be in the right headspace to hear it.

She releases a soft chuckle while perching on a stool across from mine. "You might not believe me now, but there's going to come a time when you look back and wish you two were having fights like this."

"I find that hard to believe." I get up to toss the rest of my sandwich, shaking my head at the idea.

"You would because you're still young." A smile plays at the corners of her mouth as she sets her delicate China cup onto its saucer. "Years from now, when you're bouncing grandbabies on your knee, you'll wish things were this simple again. These silly understandings only flare up when you're in the beginning together. When you have plenty of time ahead of you, you'll wish you could go back." She's not talking about me anymore, not when her gaze is unfocused and there's sadness hanging in her voice. Regret, maybe.

My chest goes tight, forcing me to address the obvious as I slowly approach her. "Mama. Tell me the truth. What's wrong with Papa? Is he sick?"

She may as well be a robot following instructions, sitting up straighter, smiling unnaturally. The warmth in her eyes has melted away, replaced by a pale imitation. The way you smile when you're trying to be polite or avoid hurting someone's feelings. Not that I've ever wasted much time with that, but she excels at it. "What would give you that idea? You're too much like me. You worry about things when you feel like you're out of control in other areas. Don't do that to yourself."

Then she stands, making my heart sink as I watch her move slowly to grab the sugar bowl from the other end of the island like there's an invisible weight dragging her down. There's nothing I can do but wish she would share with me, but then I have no doubt she's been forbidden against it by Papa.

"I've been meaning to ask you a favor," I tell her. Originally, this was supposed to be about Emilia and me, but now it might also serve to take Mama's mind off of Papa since I've clearly upset her. "I was thinking about going to the house in the Hamptons for a week. Someplace quiet where she can enjoy a little more freedom. I'll still be in contact, but she needs a change of scenery, and you know we have a team in case we need them, which I doubt we will." *And we could use some time to ourselves.*

"Of course she does." Mama wears a radiant smile again as she stirs her tea. "That's a wonderful idea. Certainly, it shouldn't take more than a day's notice to have the place ready for you."

"I doubt Dante will think it's wonderful," I point out, imagining his shitty reaction, but I can't bring myself to care enough to change my mind.

"I'll deal with him," she promises, and I don't have the heart to snicker when she looks happy. She has much more faith in him than I do. Then again, I'm sure he feels the same way when it comes to me. My mother and I have always had a special connection, and it's always pissed him off.

"For now..." Mama concludes, "... you go back down to your house, you apologize, and you tell her you were the world's biggest idiot for getting angry. You tell her you'll do anything she needs. *Capisci*?" she adds, narrowing her eyes.

"*Capisco*." I know better than to argue, even if it won't be as easy as throwing myself on my knees and begging.

I don't beg.

It's not in my nature.

Still, I have to do something. Every fucking minute without Emilia is torture.

13

EMILIA

My eyes are so swollen after hours of weeping I can barely open them when I wake up.

I left the bedroom curtains parted a crack so I'd wake with the sun in case Luca didn't come back by dawn. While the idea of going up to the house doesn't inspire good feelings, I decided to do it as a last-ditch effort if he was still up there.

Considering I'm alone in bed, it looks like I'll have to swallow my pride and head up. I can't sit here and wait all day like last night. It's absurd. It hurts too much.

My eyes hurt as I splash my face in the bathroom sink, the cold water tingling my skin. It at least tricks me into feeling more alert. It doesn't make my face look less puffy, though. The sight of my reflection is damn near horrific after I spent the night tossing and turning before finally falling into a light sleep full of nightmares.

How could he stay away all night? How does he not care? The questions make me grind my teeth as I quickly brush them, then turn my rat's nest into something that looks more like human hair.

It was a rough night. Was it for both of us?

I have my answer when I leave the bedroom and find Luca asleep on the couch. My heart skips a beat while tears fill my eyes at the sight of him. He stripped down to his boxer briefs, leaving his suit lying over the back of a chair.

He'd rather sleep out here than with me? Somehow, that hurts worst of all.

My freshly wounded heart propels me across the room so I can place a hand on his bare shoulder and shake gently. "Hey. When did you come back?" I whisper hesitantly.

His eyes snap open wide so suddenly I jump back a step while he sits up part way, looking around wildly before relaxing. "Overnight. You were in bed. I didn't want to wake you." He sits up the rest of the way and sets his feet on the floor, scrubbing his hands over his scruffy cheeks, then letting them fall to his lap.

My hands, meanwhile, are clenched together behind my back. I'm trying to navigate uncharted territory. There's no guessing how this is going to go. "For future reference, don't ever worry about waking me up. I probably would've slept a lot better if I had known you came home," I point out, stifling a yawn.

"Right," he murmurs, staring down at his lap. "I didn't think about it that way." If only I knew what he's thinking and feeling. He's speaking slowly as if he is weighing every word with care. My chest hurts a little more with every heavy heartbeat. I can't take it anymore. One of us has to break the ice.

"I'm sorry," I blurt out. "I should've been upfront with you instead of keeping everything to myself, but you must know... I didn't want to hurt you or make you think I was ashamed or anything. I'm not. It's just so tricky."

He blows out a sigh that puffs out his cheeks, falling

back on the cushions and patting his lap. "Come here." I do as he asks without hesitating since what I need more than anything right now is to be close to him. Curling up in his lap, his arms pull me close to his chest, and a feeling of peace settles over me. Finally, I'm back where I belong, my head resting on his shoulder.

"I'm not good at this shit," he grumbles after a heavy silence. "Relationships and talking. There's a reason I never got into any of this. I'm going to suck at communicating, or whenever you want to call it. When you're used to fighting your way through everything and not really giving a shit over what anybody thinks, it's a tough habit to break."

"I understand that." Touching a hand to his chest, I feel the steady beat of his heart. I've gotten used to hearing it under my ear when I fall asleep, and its absence deepened my misery last night.

He chuckles softly, covering my hand with his. "I wouldn't give a shit except I fucking do."

"That's true." I would agree to anything right now. Being close to him again is too important to risk ruining the moment. It's not like he doesn't make a good point. I'd rather be with somebody who cares passionately than someone who can shrug and walk away without putting up a fight.

"What I'm trying to say is, be patient with me. I'm trying, even when it doesn't seem that way." He lifts my hand and presses his lips against my palm. "I'll do better from now on."

"And I'm so sorry," I whisper as emotion rises in my chest. It clogs my throat, cutting off the rest of my apology while I fight back tears. That's not what I want this to be about, him comforting me through a sob fest.

"You don't have to apologize. That's one thing you do not

have to do." Taking my face in his hands, his eyes search mine, and I see desperation and fear in his. "I wasn't thinking, but I am now. It wasn't fair to expect you to shrug everything off and announce us to your parents without easing into it. Obviously, we'll have to be careful."

"We?" I ask, almost afraid to hope he's giving me everything I want.

"Yes, we. That's what it's all about. I'm here for you, whatever you need. All you have to do is name it. We'll figure this out together," he vows, kissing me until my tears wet our cheeks, and we're both breathless.

"I didn't know until now that that was all I needed you to say," I confess with a teary laugh. "I just don't want you to hate me because of it."

"Not possible." He smiles sheepishly, tucking hair behind my ears, then wiping my cheeks with his thumbs. "I've been thinking. You need a break. A longer one, more than a night out somewhere. We could use time on our own too."

Who am I to argue? "What did you have in mind?"

"How about a week in the Hamptons?" he inquires like it's an everyday thing.

I didn't expect him to be able to rattle off an answer like that. I figured this was sort of a hypothetical thing. "The Hamptons?" I ask since I'm pretty sure I didn't hear him correctly.

"We have a vacation house there. I already spoke to Mama about it, and she'll make sure the place is ready for us. It's off-season, meaning it'll be quieter, and we'll have more freedom to wander around like so-called normal people."

I'm still reeling from the surprise when he kisses the tip

of my nose. "And maybe we'll hammer out a plan for how to move forward with your parents while we're up there. A little time in front of the fire and a dip in the heated pool, and we might be able to think a little clearer."

"You had me at heated pool," I tell him, throwing my arms around his neck while he laughs. A whole week away together. No family drama, no mafia war, nothing but the two of us. My heart is ready to soar. "So long as you're sure it's the right time for you to be away."

"You're going to have to let me worry about that," he murmurs in my ear while rubbing my back. "You worry about what to bring with you. As far as I'm concerned, you don't have to wear any clothes. If you want to go out in public, you might want to pack a few outfits."

"If I have to..." I say, giggling when he growls. God, I love that sound.

Then he sighs, squeezing me again before loosening his grip so I can scramble out of his lap. "I need a shower and half a pot of coffee injected straight into my veins if there's a hope of getting out of here for a week without getting my ass handed to me," he grumbles. Stretching, he adds, "Let's shoot for leaving tomorrow. The sooner we're out of here, the better."

The way he makes it sound, he needs this as much as I do. I imagine Dante will complain about his brother ducking out while so much is happening. No doubt Luca has that in mind when he groans his way through getting up and walking to the bathroom.

"I'll make coffee," I offer. It's amazing how much brighter the world seems now. Luca is back. We have a plan to move forward and a week in the Hamptons to look forward to. Once I've set the coffee to brew, I take a deep breath and send a quick text to Mom.

Me: *I'm going away for a week on a last-minute trip. When I come back, we'll have dinner together. I have lots of good news to share.*

I only need to convince her and Dad that this is good news.

14

LUCA

"That should cover everything." I step back from my father's desk and glance around the room. Francesco and Niccolo don't wear much of an expression at all. It doesn't matter to them that I plan on *running off for a week*, as my brother not so kindly put it. Probably because they're not heartless assholes like he is.

Either that, or it's because they don't hate me the way he does.

"We'll keep you in the loop," Papa promises with a faint smile. He sounds stronger today, which helps a lot. I doubt I'd be able to stop worrying about him if he looked like hell before I left. "Go on, show the girl a nice time. Your mother and I spoke about this, and we agree it's the right thing to do."

Dante doesn't bother disguising his bitterness, though even I'm surprised when he blurts out a laugh at Papa's statement. Our father lifts his brows, and I can understand why. "Did I say anything funny?" he asks, tipping his head to the side and looking Dante up and down. "Please, let me know. Maybe I can laugh along with you." Most full-grown men would find themselves on the verge of pissing their pants if the notorious Rocco Santoro asked that question. Hell, even Cesco squirms a little, then exchanges a glance with Nico.

Dante squares his shoulders. "Pardon me, but I have to say something. Am I living in an alternate reality where any of this makes sense?" When Papa only stares at him, Dante barks out another laugh and then continues his tirade. "The entire reason she's here is because he can't live without her, and now he's going away for a week's vacation when there are gun fights breaking out on the streets, and two of our strongest allies have lost business thanks to Vitali lashing out at them."

He's smirking when he turns to me. "But by all means, turn a blind eye. Think only about yourself and whether you'll get your dick wet," he concludes.

"I'm going to the Hampton house," I remind him, forcing out every word when I'd much rather strangle the life out of him. "I'm not flying to Miami or LA, for fuck's sake. If something happens, it'll be easy to reach me, and you know it."

"Fine, you want to be a stubborn prick about it? Let me remind you that you were almost assassinated barely a week and a half ago at the club. The club you swear is so fucking secure. Who's to say something like that won't happen while you're away?" He's so goddamn superior in his own mind. It would be funny if it weren't so sad.

Nico clears his throat. "The club will be fine," he offers, staring at Dante with no expression. Anyone who knows my cousin knows he's at his most dangerous when he's this calm, meaning my brother is treading on thin ice. "There are two more bouncers with handheld metal detectors. Nobody's slipping past again."

"Don't pretend you're really concerned about the club." I

grunt. "You're pissy because, unlike you, I've got a life outside all of this. Sorry if you can't understand the need to do things for other people. If you'd pull your head out of your ass—"

His eyes fly open wide. "Doing things for other people? That's all I ever fucking do," Dante fires back, leaping out of his chair and glaring at me like he's dying to hurt me. I couldn't be happier. All I need is an excuse to take a swing at him, and he looks like he's ready to go.

"Stop, for fuck's sake." Papa doesn't have it in him to raise his voice, though somehow, his disappointment rings out louder the quieter he gets. "Dante, you seem to forget I still have final say around here, and I say your brother needs to take his girl away. She's been true to her word so far. No trouble. She keeps to herself. We hardly know she's here. She needs a little time away. If positions were switched, I would be just as much in favor of you getting out of here for a while."

"The positions would never be switched," Dante insists while glaring at me. "I wouldn't put us in this position in the first place." *Because he can't find a woman charitable enough to fuck him.*

"Congratulations," I reply, giving him a slow golf clap that makes his face go red. "You win. You're the good son."

"Go," Papa mutters, waving a hand and cutting off Dante's reply. "Before I change my mind and have you stay. Maybe you'll come back with a better attitude."

It isn't my attitude that needs fixing, but I'm not about to waste more time. Every minute spent bickering with my brother is one less I get to spend with Emilia. She's waiting for me, and anticipation makes my heart pound a little faster as I leave the house to find the car already here.

Bruno and Pete are coming with us, staying in the guest

house out by the pool. I'm not about to take any chances, no matter how quiet I expect the trip to be. At least, quiet in terms of interruptions from anyone who wants to see me dead. I intend to christen every room and test the acoustics when Emilia screams my name.

She comes bouncing out of my house, practically skipping toward the waiting car when she finds me beside it, giving the guys last-minute instructions. "Ready to go?" I ask, holding my arms out so she can throw herself into them. All of the bullshit with Dante falls away in a moment like this.

This is what is real.

This is what matters.

"So ready." Her radiant smile turns wicked as she molds her body against mine. "There's only one tiny problem."

"What is it?"

"I don't have a bathing suit. I guess I won't be able to wear one while we're in the pool." Her teeth scrape her lip as she raises an eyebrow. "I don't know what we're going to do."

Note to self, get in the pool right away. "I'm sure we'll be able to come up with a way around that," I promise, my dick thickening in anticipation. "We need to get moving. I don't think I can wait much longer."

Good thing it's less than an hour's drive up there.

"This is your *vacation* home?" I have the pleasure of watching Emilia gape in amazement as we enter the house, which even I can agree is breathtaking. I've grown used to it over the years, but she helps me see things through new eyes. I can better appreciate the sprawling mansion situated only yards from the beach, the windows that allow so much brilliant sunlight to stream into the open, airy space.

My mother was true to her word, ensuring the place was open and aired out and the kitchen stocked. The pool is ready for us, too, beneath the enclosure Papa built for Guilia a decade ago so she could swim year-round. What a shame we've been too busy to come up here much recently.

"You like it?" I ask, though the answer is obvious.

She might as well roll her eyes at my question. "It's incredible. I've seen pictures of houses like this." She's almost tiptoeing through the space, running her fingertips over the striped sofa positioned before the wide, deep fireplace. Going to the windows, she shakes her head and even laughs softly. "Right on the beach. Like it's straight out of a magazine." Then she turns to me, eyes shining. "Thank you so much for bringing me here. Thank you for thinking about this."

"It was nothing," I offer with a shrug, taking off my coat and hanging it with hers near the front door while she admires our surroundings. "The house just happens to be here."

"You thought of bringing me here." She joins me at the foot of the stairs and winds her arms around my waist. Radiant, loving, and tempting. Even now, in a sweet moment like this, I can't wait to tear off her clothes.

If only we could shut out the world all the time, to live in a bubble where there's nothing but the two of us, and I could have her all to myself.

"I think of a lot of things," I murmur, letting one of my hands slide down her back until I'm cupping her ass. She glances toward the guys, currently coming in with our bags, but I don't care if they see us. I hope they do. Just in case they ever get the stupid idea to touch what isn't theirs. What is *mine*.

"Take them up to the front bedroom," I call out, leading her farther into the house. Bruno is carrying my bag, and I make a point of catching his eye, adding, "Leave mine in the closet." There's something special inside that I'd rather Emilia not accidentally discover. Something I plan to give her this week. My chest tightens every time I think about it.

"You're going to have to take me on a tour," Emilia reminds me, taking me by the hand and bringing my thoughts back to the present. "I want to see everything."

"Same here, which is why I was thinking about having a swim," I murmur with a wink. Emilia's cheeks go pink, but she rolls her eyes, making me relent. "Okay, fine," I grumble.

She whistles at the sight of the expansive, well-stocked library. "I could spend a month in here," she decides with a happy little sigh before we continue to the kitchen. "It's more like a cathedral!" Craning her neck, she gazes at the ceiling far above our heads.

"The guy who built it was going for shock and awe." That's not what I'm interested in. I would much rather pull her through the French doors leading to the pool. It's clear, sparkling water looks inviting enough that I'd want to swim even without the prospect of a slippery, naked woman joining me.

Finally, she finishes checking out the shining appliances, practically moaning over the array of treats in the refrigerator. Mama made a point of spoiling us, to put it mildly. I make a mental note to thank her for it while pulling Emilia outside.

"Wow. The parties we could have out here." She shakes her head, grinning from ear to ear at the attached glass-walled enclosure that lets in the late morning sunshine and gives us the illusion of being outside, though we're fully protected from the bracing wind coming off the ocean.

"You're reading my mind," I tell her while opening the control pad on the wall beside the door and touching the button, lowering the shades over the windows to give us privacy.

She turns to me, folding her arms and smirking. "I told you..." she reminds me in a teasing sort of voice, "... I didn't bring a suit."

"And wouldn't you know it, neither did I." The hem of my turtleneck is already in my hands, and I pull it over my head, tossing it onto one of the lounge chairs positioned around the pool's edge. "That's not stopping me, is it?"

Wearing a wry grin, she slides out of her flats, then dips a toe into the water. "It does feel nice," she announces.

"What do you say?" I ask, kicking off my shoes and then peeling off my socks. My gaze never leaves hers as I work on my belt next, and her teeth sink into her bottom lip. The action does nothing to hide a naughty smile. "How about we start this trip off the right way?" I suggest with a smile that mirrors hers.

She pretends to resist for another three seconds before giving in. "If you insist." Suddenly, her sweater is lying on the floor, soon joined by her bra. I watch, my breath quickening with every layer she peels away until she dives gracefully into the deep end.

When she surfaces, her hair is slicked back, and she's laughing. "It's fantastic! Hurry up and get in here, Luca!"

As if I needed an invitation.

15

EMILIA

It's like living in a dream. The sweetest, most perfect dream imaginable.

I'm sort of sad two days have already passed, but there are still five to go when I wake up in Luca's arms, wrapped in a soft, down comforter and practically floating on the most comfortable bed imaginable. I've slept like a baby since we arrived. I never knew it made such a difference in the bed a person used.

There I was, thinking I grew up comfortably—which I did, having a lawyer for a father—but I sure as hell never knew it was possible to live like this.

I realize the bed isn't all there is to it once I identify what's now become a familiar sound. The bedroom features tall French doors that open onto a balcony overlooking Main Beach and the water beyond it. The sound of waves crashing against the shore has lulled me to sleep every night. I can see myself spending summers here, living by the rhythms of nature, waking with the sun, and having my coffee out on the balcony where I can drink in every sound, every sparkle on the water's surface.

Luca is still asleep, but damn, I don't want to waste a minute here. We can sleep in at home, where there isn't a gorgeous beach waiting to be walked along. After taking a minute to admire how his skin glows in the morning sunshine, I press a soft kiss against his scruffy cheek. "Good morning," I whisper, smiling when he does. "Come with me for a walk on the beach. Maybe we can go to that little café we saw yesterday and get some breakfast."

His eyes are still closed when he releases a growl. "I was thinking we could get our exercise in other ways this morning," he murmurs as his hand slides down my back.

"Oh, we'll still do that," I promise, placing a long, lingering kiss against his lips and giggling when his eyes snap open. There are few surefire ways to get his attention, but this is one of them.

Trying to take a nice morning walk when bodyguards are following us is a little awkward. I can't exactly forget they exist, even though I try to do just that as we walk with our arms around each other's waists, admiring the guys in wetsuits who are somehow crazy enough to surf in the cold. One of them stands at the water's edge and clearly stares at the men tailing us before shrugging and turning away. Considering the size of the other homes lining the beach, I can't imagine we're the only people in need of a little protection sometimes.

It's the same in the village, where we manage to have breakfast while tucked away in the corner of a charming café, almost like being an average, everyday couple, except for the presence of the two burly men waiting for us a few tables over.

"I've been thinking." Once Luca has finished plowing through his stack of banana walnut pancakes, he pushes the rest aside and folds his arms on the table. "Let's do something special tonight."

I'm still too busy having a love affair with my stuffed French toast to think about the future. "I thought this whole week was special," I point out, taking another bite and trying not to moan out loud.

But the sight of him doesn't make it any easier. He is so damn handsome in his cream-colored turtleneck, which sets off his dark coloring to perfection. "I know, but I wanted to do something a little extra for you."

I reach across the table and squeeze his hand. "You're already doing so much." I'm sure memories of what he left behind have to be weighing on him, even if he keeps it to himself. Dante has called at least three times that I'm aware of, and I caught little bits and pieces of Luca's side of a tense argument last night before we went to dinner.

There's no hint of that in his easy smile. It still has the power to take my breath away. "I'm the one who decides if I'm doing too much, and I haven't come close yet. I want you to treat yourself today. I want you to go to the salon around the corner from here and have your hair done, nails, pedicure... whatever you want. Pull out all the stops."

The idea leaves me fighting back a laugh. "I can't just walk in, even if it is off-season," I remind him. Only a man would think it's that simple.

Then again, this is not any ordinary man. "I already called and let them know you'd be coming in, and they understand the sky's the limit. Whatever you want." He sits back in his chair, arms folded, smirking at my surprise.

"What!" I gasp. "That's... Luca! You're spoiling me, you know that?"

His thick shoulders lift. "No such thing. And even if I was, it would only be because you deserve it."

"What are you going to be doing while I'm so busy getting pampered?" At the slight creasing of his brow, I realize it's the wrong question. He probably has phone calls to make and business to be done. God forbid we should have a week to ourselves, but I need to be realistic. He's always going to be a busy man.

"Don't you worry about that." He signals for the check, then has a silent conversation with the guys before they head outside to wait for us. It's like they can read his thoughts. "You are under strict instruction to spoil yourself today. Pete will follow you, and he has my card. Do a little shopping afterward, get yourself something nice. We're going to have a special dinner tonight."

My head is spinning by the time we get up from the table. "I can hardly wait." He helps me put on my coat, then settles the bill while I step outside to wait. As usual, the bodyguards don't bother saying anything to me. They only nod respectfully, then hold the typical murmured conversation.

"All right, go on now," Luca urges when he joins us, then jerks his chin at Pete before reverting his gaze to me. "We'll have to work on our exercise when you get back," he adds in a softer voice, full of meaning.

"Then I'll make sure to hurry back when I'm finished." We're both grinning happily before we share a soft, lingering kiss. He tastes like coffee and syrup, and I would love to indulge him some more.

Still, it's been a while since I've had a trim, come to think of it, and even longer since my last mani-pedi. It's amazing how I hadn't considered having any of this done in the past, but now I can't wait to get to the salon.

As it turns out, there are perks to this lifestyle. I was so hesitant to indulge back when I first went shopping with

Guilia, and now I'm happily anticipating a little pampering. Maybe I am finally getting used to this.

By the time I leave the boutique with a bag in hand, hours after parting ways with Luca, I feel like a new woman. My freshly painted nails stand out a vibrant red against the white handles, and I can't help but flip my freshly blown-out waves over my shoulders as I walk back to the house. Every time I pass a window, I have to look and admire.

Considering Luca's eyeballs nearly fall out of his head when I walk into the living room, I'd say it was well worth it. "You look incredible. Holy shit." He looks me up and down, smiling as he crosses the room and takes hold of me. "Forget my plans for tonight. We're gonna stay right here in front of the fireplace."

"Need anything else right now, boss?" Pete asks, and Luca dismisses him. I thank him for escorting me as he heads over to the guest house, which is bigger than some of the homes my friends lived in back in high school. Everything the Santoro family does is on a grand scale.

Luca is on me the instant we're alone, pawing at my clothes with his face buried against my neck. "Fuck, you smell good. What did they use on your hair? I'm going to have to buy you a lifetime supply," he groans out.

"I'm afraid you would never be able to get anything else done if you did."

His hands are already under my sweater, working the hooks on my bra. "Maybe I'll retire early," he decides, pulling my hips tight against him, squeezing my ass as he backs me up until we're in front of the fireplace, where a thick throw rug lays. He pulls me down until we're on our knees. I'm wet, my heart is racing with anticipation, and I'm just as eager to get him out of his clothes as he is to get me out of mine.

"So fucking beautiful." As soon as my sweater is over my head, he pulls my bra away, cupping my breasts and lifting them as he lowers his head to close his lips around one nipple. Then he moves to the other while I run my fingers through his hair and claw at his back.

"Oh God," I moan out when he scrapes his teeth over my sensitive flesh.

"I like the sound of that." His dark eyes flash with desire as he lowers me to my back, and I lift my hips so he can take off my jeans, trembling in anticipation. "Calling me God is something I could get used to."

My giggling is cut short by the sweep of his tongue over my lower belly, then he takes the waistband of my thong in his teeth and begins slipping it down my legs. Propping myself on my elbows, I watch him, completely wrapped up in the erotic sight. He takes his time, building the already unbearable tension. When he glances up at me, the heat in his eyes tells me he's craving me. The animal is beneath the surface, one he's barely in control of.

Then, with a growl, he tosses the thong aside and forces my legs as far apart as I can get them before feasting on me. There's nothing to do but fall back with a moan and give myself to him.

"SHIT."

I barely stir myself from the drowsiness, lifting my head from his chest. "What? What's wrong?" I ask in a voice thick with sleep.

"I just saw the clock on the mantle." He groans. "You have a way of making me lose track of time."

I look up from the nest of throw blankets he made after I

screamed the house down earlier. The clock reads six forty-five. "No way," I mumble, even though it shouldn't come as a surprise. Night has fallen between my third and final orgasm and now. "We've been here for hours. I didn't think I fell asleep."

"I'm going to need you to do something for me." He sits up like he's in a hurry, kissing my forehead before standing. "I'm going to head up and take a quick shower, and then I have a couple of appointments I need to keep. I'll be back by eight. When I get here, I expect you to be ready."

"Ready for what?" I ask, wrapping one of the blankets around me as we gather our clothes from where we discarded them all over the room, then head upstairs.

"For our special night," he reminds me. "You did buy something special today, I assume?"

He has no idea. The anticipation of his reaction makes my pulse pick up speed. "Yep. I can't wait to try it on for you."

"I can't wait to see it." He's already in the bathroom but leaves the door open while turning on the shower. "I'll be back at eight like I said. On the dot."

"I'll be ready," I promise. Whatever this is all about, it's important enough to make Lucas obsess over me being ready on time. I'm the first person to admit I am not always punctual when it comes to preparing for a special night, but it's not like I make it a habit of being late.

As soon as he leaves, I clip my hair up and draw a hot bath, soaking in the deep tub for twenty minutes. When I catch a look at myself in the mirror, the smile I'm wearing makes it grow wider. I'm happy and completely in love.

If only it could always be like this. If only we could live here forever, away from the family and danger. We could be so happy here for the rest of our lives. I'm sure of it.

Finishing my sexy smoky eye makeup, I shimmy into the short, tight, red dress I bought for the occasion. It's sexy as hell, only falling halfway down my thighs, held up with thin straps. He'll love the low-cut neckline. I would never consider anything like this if it wasn't for him, knowing how he would react. I bought a black cashmere cardigan to go over it in case we're actually going someplace tonight, and I want to look somewhat presentable, but for now, I'll leave it off to give him the full effect.

After sliding into a pair of black stilettos, I step back from the mirror and chew my lip, checking myself out one last time. He'll be here in around fifteen minutes. At least he won't be able to say I'm taking too long getting ready.

As if by magic, his footsteps ring out downstairs while I'm thinking about him. "You're early!" I shout, laughing. "But the joke's on you. I'm ready, just like you wanted me to be."

He doesn't answer. "Luca?" I call out, and before the name is even out of my mouth, I want to slap myself. "Sorry. Pete? Bruno? Everything okay?"

The silence that follows chills my blood.

Something is wrong.

And I have no way of defending myself.

Maybe I was hearing things. We're completely safe here. Nobody even knows we came up for the week. No way would Luca have let me wander around freely today, even with a bodyguard, had he suspected trouble on the horizon.

But I heard those footsteps, and now I feel something. A tingle along the back of my neck, goose bumps covering my arms and legs as I take one slow step after another into the hall until I'm standing at the top of the stairs. From what I can see, the living room is empty, as we left it.

A floorboard creaks downstairs.

Shit!

All of my training comes rushing back. There is an intruder. I need to get help. The closest thing to a weapon I have on me is the heels of my shoes. I slip them off, one eye always on the expanse of the living room visible from where I'm standing.

What can I do? A few possibilities race through my mind all at once. My phone is in the bedroom. I could go back and get it, call Luca, and beg him to come home. How long would that take? I don't have Pete's or Bruno's numbers. Dammit.

Where are they? How could somebody break in without them knowing?

I could run down the stairs and out the front door. It wouldn't take long if I ran without stopping. I might be able to beat whoever is here, run outside, and scream my head off. But what if somebody's waiting out there?

I could run for the kitchen and grab a knife, but that would take too long. I could hide and wait for Luca to get back. Ten minutes or so, right? It would feel like ten hours. A lot can happen in that amount of time.

I place one bare foot on the first step, holding my breath. Silence. Another step. Another. I can see the front door now. It's probably my best bet. I hold the shoes in front of me, prepared to jam the heels through somebody's neck.

Halfway down the stairs, there's another creak. This time, louder. Closer.

A burst of adrenaline propels me the rest of the way, my feet flying over the stairs. By the time I reach the first floor, a dark shape looms in the corner of my eye, but that only gets me moving faster.

Until a second dark shape throws itself in front of the door, blocking the way. I barely have time to halt my forward motion before a steel band loops around my waist from behind, and the stench of cheap cologne threatens to choke me.

I don't take time to get a look at my attacker. Reflex takes over, and I slam my elbow into his ribs, then take advantage of him doubling over and drive the same elbow into his eye as hard as I can.

"Bitch!" he shouts but lets me go. Only for his partner to lunge at me. I swing with the heel of my shoe and make contact with his cheek, tearing his flesh, but his pained cry only seems to give him added strength and determination. He hits me low, driving his head into my midsection and knocking the wind from my lungs. I stagger back and fall against the stairs, kicking when he descends on me.

"Fucking cunt!" He snarls, ignoring my kicks and screams as he takes me by the shoulders and slams my head against the step beneath it.

16

LUCA

"Can you go back and confirm for me? I'm trying to keep a schedule here, and I need to know that everything is in place before I head home." This is the kindest I've been in a long time, but there's too much riding on tonight to blow it all up by losing my shit on a restaurant hostess. It isn't easy to keep from asking the girl exactly how the hell she manages to do her job when she can't understand simple instructions. This has long been my family's favorite restaurant in the Hamptons. It seemed like a surefire thing, but I'm starting to wonder as I watch the girl hustle through the dining room on her way to the kitchen.

"Good luck," a man mutters nearby. "All I did was ask for a quart of lobster bisque to go, and I got some bullshit line about the kitchen being short-staffed and how I'd have to wait."

Strange, but the voice sounds vaguely familiar. I turn to find someone I didn't notice when I came in, most likely because I'm completely focused on everything being perfect tonight. "Barrett Black!" I realize, laughing when I recognize a friend of mine. "No shit. How are you? You're looking

good." We exchange a firm handshake, stepping aside so
we're not in the way of anybody coming in.

I first got to know Barrett through his construction business when I was pricing contractors during the club's expan-
sion and renovation, and while we don't run in the same
circles, we make it a point to keep in touch. He's also visited
the club with his wealthy friends a few times, though his
recent marriage has changed his social habits.

"I can't complain," he tells me, wearing an easy grin.
"Though I am a little disappointed at the moment. Is the
kitchen too short-staffed to ladle out some soup? When does
that happen?"

"Since I hired them to cook and serve at my house
tonight." I wouldn't normally brag. It's not in my nature, and
I've always found braggarts to be the people with the least to
brag about. Every once in a while, though, it's worth it.

For instance, when Barrett's mouth falls open before he
can help it, "Nice move. I'll tell my wife she has you to thank
if I'm not able to satisfy her pregnancy craving."

"Tough luck," I offer, wincing. I've dealt with some fairly
intimidating characters in my time, but I'm not sure I would
get in the way of a pregnant woman.

"So long as I know who to point her toward if she's
pissed," he says with a shrug.

"Mr. Santoro? Everything is in place, and they're loading
your order into the delivery van now." I don't know which of
us is more relieved, me or the hostess, as she returns to her
stand.

"Thanks." I shake Barrett's hand again and promise to
touch base when we're home. It's the sort of promise people
make whether or not they believe there's any chance of
making good on it.

I do hope to meet his wife, Lourde, who might be

someone Emilia would get along with. Eventually, there will come a time for us to live in the world together instead of being secluded. I want her to have a social life if that's what she needs.

With everything in place, I head out to the car to drive back to the house. I'll distract Emilia upstairs while the staff from the restaurant and the florist set up the downstairs. I wanted to fill the first floor with roses since the ones at home made her so happy. I sure as hell spent enough on them, but then there's no such thing as too much when it comes to her.

The velvet box in my pants pocket gets heavier the closer I come to the house. I planned to ask after dinner, though now I wonder if I shouldn't get it over with. I don't know if I'll be able to enjoy the meal, running through what I want to say in my head.

I can't believe I'm this nervous. It's crazy what she does to me. I'm practically beside myself with anticipation. She'll say yes. I know she will. That doesn't mean I don't want everything to be as perfect as she deserves. I want her to remember this night for the rest of her life.

It's almost eight now. Emilia will be ready, waiting for me, though she doesn't know she's waiting for something else. Something we both want.

Forever.

It's the open door that stops me as I pull up. The sight of it flips a switch in my head. The anxious, lovesick fool is gone, and in his place is the man I was before I ever set eyes on Emilia Washington. As if on autopilot, I reach into the glove box and pull out the Glock, checking to make sure the safety is off. Then I get out and jog up to the porch, taking in everything.

"Emilia?" The house is silent and dark. I reach inside far

enough to turn on the lights, and my gaze is immediately drawn to a black stiletto lying on the floor in front of the stairs. The second one lies on the third stair.

The smear of blood dripping down the riser above makes the world stop turning.

In the blink of an eye, everything changes. A heart-stopping moment of panic sets in as I take the steps two at a time, shouting all the way. "Emilia! If you're here, tell me where you are!" A quick search of the bedrooms yields nothing.

"Emilia!" I rush down the stairs, and now headlights are sweeping over the front courtyard. The fucking florist. I run out, waving my arms. "Don't go in!" I bark without slowing my pace, heading for the guest house. I know what I'm going to find before I make it there. There is no way Emilia is missing from this house unless somebody has already taken care of them.

By the time I reach the door, an icy sweat coats my skin, and I'm pretty sure I'm losing my mind. It doesn't get any better when I find the corpses of my bodyguards sitting at the kitchen table, both of them face down with half of their heads missing and their brains splattered on the wall beside them. They were having dinner. One of the windows across from the table is blown in from the outside, glass littering the floor. Motherfuckers had the audacity to walk straight up to the window and fire.

I take it all in, then run back to the house. By now, the restaurant crew waits with the florists, everybody standing around, looking anxious.

"Get out of here, everybody. The plan has changed. You've all been paid, so go." Their confused, surprised objections ring out behind me, but it's about as important as the buzzing of a gnat in my ear. Back inside, the bloodstain glares sickeningly against the white paint. It's an accusation.

You couldn't keep me safe.

You were never good enough for me.

My hands shake with helpless rage as I pull out my phone, hitting the contact for my father's cell while quickly searching the first floor in case I'm missing something. There is nothing beyond the broken lock on a door leading out to the beach. The alarm wasn't set. Why didn't I tell her to set the alarm? Why didn't I do it myself? Because the guards were outside, that's why, and I would only be gone for an hour. Because this wasn't supposed to fucking happen.

"Papa," I bark when he answers. "He took her. He fucking took her."

"I know." His resigned sigh almost drowns out my gasp of sick surprise. "There was a call to the main house number a few minutes ago. They said they had something that belongs to you, and they'll get in touch when the time is right. I told myself it was a prank if you hadn't already called here."

Now he knows better. My world is crumbling around me, and the most precious thing I've ever known is out there somewhere, needing me. "He has her. Papa, he has her." I can't stop saying it. I can barely hear myself over the roaring in my head.

"Come home," he urges. "Come home, and we'll get her back."

Yes, we will, but that won't be enough.

I won't be satisfied until the flesh is peeled from his bones while he watches on in horror.

17

EMILIA

Everything hurts.

My body is a symphony of pain.

What a first thought to have when regaining consciousness. But it's true. I'm aching from head to toe, shivering before registering the unforgiving cold I'm in. The throbbing in the back of my skull is the worst, consuming most of my attention, but virtually every joint is throbbing.

But I'm alive. Freezing but alive.

And alone.

I ease one eyelid open enough to identify that much, and the absence of breathing when I hold mine is a pretty good indicator. The only sound is something dripping somewhere, like a leaky pipe. The steady *plink-plink* is unnerving, much like this entire situation.

Inventory time. I can move everything. There doesn't seem to be any broken bones to worry about. Pressing my hands against the surface I'm lying on tells me there's a mattress under me. Old, by the smell of it, sort of musty and dank.

Someone could be watching me, which is all that keeps

me from trying to sit up and examine the space. I have to keep every possibility in mind, like playing chess with an invisible partner.

There's not a doubt in my mind who is behind this. I'm sure of that much, not that the certainty brings me any comfort. Alessandro Vitali is vicious on a level the Santoros haven't approached.

A bare bulb hanging in one corner provides the only light in the room, giving me just enough to see by once I've eased my eyes open to take in what's probably a basement somewhere, with a small window positioned high up on the wall. It's narrow enough that there'd be no hope of squeezing through and probably painted shut from the looks of it. A windowless door is embedded in one cinder block wall, positioned a few feet from the foot of my bed. It's still dark outside, so unless I slept an entire day away, it's only been a matter of hours since I ended up here.

Luca must be going crazy. Out of everything going through my head as I lie on this old mattress, that's the worst. Knowing he's suffering. He probably thinks I'm dead already, and my throat closes up before I can help it. I can't afford to lose myself to panic or worry. I have to conserve my energy, both physical and emotional. Nothing has ever mattered more.

The door might look heavy and solid, but it doesn't do much to block out the sound of heavy footsteps on the other side. My heart seizes, and I go still, listening hard, ready to fight again if it comes to it. I doubt I would get very far, but I'll be damned if I will make it easy for them.

"Boss says she's awake," somebody mutters close to the door.

"I'll have to thank her for this black eye," another voice grumbles. My fist curls on its own when I remember driving my elbow into somebody's eye. Good. I hope he can't see out of it for a week.

"You remember what he said," his friend insists. "Not yet." I don't have time to reflect on what that might mean, not that it requires much reflection.

My eyes are closed, but I can still see the light now streaming into the room. It must be pretty bright out there. Something hits the floor that sounds metallic and maybe hollow from how the sound rings out. Fresh, icy fear leaves me grinding my teeth to hold it back, even as I feel the attention of these two thugs as they study me.

"Hey. Hey, you. Knock it off." One of them kicks the bed frame hard enough to rock it violently. It startles me into opening my eyes. "See?" he asks his friend. "I told you. Boss said she's awake."

Which means there's a camera in here somewhere. *They're watching me,* which comes as no surprise.

"Not feeling so tough now, are you?" The thug who growls has an epic shiner, and the sight of the bruise and the swelling stirs my lips into a vindictive smile.

His hand tightens into a fist, but his buddy stops him. "You know the rules," he grunts out, and the bitterness in his voice tells me he's not a big fan of the rules. I'd bet he's also not fond of the gash running in a diagonal line down his right cheek. I have no doubt he would like a little payback.

"Don't worry," he adds, flashing a nasty smile to his pal before turning his bitter gaze my way. "It's coming soon. We just have to be patient."

"This is the part where you're supposed to be intimidating me?" I ask, looking back and forth between them. "Let me know so I can pretend to be intimidated."

"Keep it up," the man with the black eye growls out,

curling his lip in a snarl that has nothing on Luca. That's because Luca isn't merely a bully. This bully has to throw his weight around, literally, because he has no actual power.

Thinking about that widens my smile. "You know, he's going to kill you for this," I murmur smoothly, smiling up at them like we're old friends. Like I'm only trying to clue them in for their own sake.

The guy with the shiner snickers. "Save your breath." With his working eye, he looks me over, and only now am I keenly aware of my dress and how much of me it reveals. This was supposed to be for Luca, dammit. All I've managed to do is make it easier for me to freeze to death in this cold, dark place. "He can try to kill us or do whatever he wants. I guess that means we have to have all the fun we can before he does, right?"

The two share a nasty little laugh that twists my insides, but I won't show it. I'll be damned if I give them a hint of how terrified I am. Luca will find me. I know he will. There's not a doubt in my mind. He would never leave me here. He will not let them get away with it, no matter what happens to me.

How much will they be able to do in the meantime? That's the question ringing out loudest in my mind as the men ogle my nearly bare legs and breasts. And all I can do is take it and pretend not to care when I would gladly peel my skin off rather than let them look at me a second longer.

"For now..." the slashed man sneers, "... you've got your bucket there." He grins at his friend. "At least we get a little entertainment."

My entire body flushes with shame, a flush that only intensifies when they share a nasty laugh, leaving the room and slamming the door, locking it behind them.

Is Alessandro Vitali watching at this very minute? Waiting for me to break down the moment I'm alone?

I won't. If he thinks this is enough to break me into some blubbering, weepy mess, he's got another thing coming. I remind myself as I rest my head on my bent arm and shiver involuntarily that he doesn't know me at all, and everybody has their limits.

I can only pray Luca gets here before Vitali pushes me to mine.

18

LUCA

"Sit down, son," Papa urges, watching me as I pace his office. "Sit. Have a drink to steady your nerves."

His words are wasted. There's only one thing I want, one thing I see in front of me—my goal, my destination, my everything. Nothing else will do.

Which means there's only one objective. "I'll kill him. I'll fucking kill him myself. This ends here, now! We have to find him. I'd bet anything he's with her now." A growl tears its way out of me. "I'll break every fucking bone in his worthless body if he lays a finger on her."

Dante has remained silent since my arrival. For some reason, he chooses this as the moment to speak. "Are you finished?" he asks, sounding bored. "We have business to think about now."

"Are you out of your fucking mind?" I whirl on him, and something in me is glad for his asshole attitude. He's given me something tangible to hate, something here, in front of me. "You have never been good at knowing when not to push me. Let me tell you, this is *not* the time."

"Dante, please," Papa speaks but watches me because I

resume walking the perimeter of the room, my hands clenched into fists so tight my joints ache. I welcome the discomfort. I can focus on it rather than the mistakes I made to get me to this point. Was it ego or plain stupidity that made me think we were safe?

Dante yawns loudly and scrubs a hand over his face. "Maybe this is for the best."

"Get him out of here," I snap at Papa, pointing to Dante. "I'll fucking kill him."

"Would you listen for once?" Dante demands, raising his voice to be heard over mine. "Let's face it. It was never right to begin with. She doesn't belong here. I can accept you getting involved with her, but she has cost this family dearly."

I used to think of my brother as nothing but a soulless machine. I was nowhere near the truth. A machine isn't cruel on purpose. "You need to leave before I kill you," I warn in a shaking voice. "I'm serious. If you can't fucking pretend to understand what I'm going through or at least muster up a little sympathy for an innocent civilian, I don't want to have shit to do with you." I don't care if we share blood. Blood means nothing to me if it means nothing to him.

"If she's suffering now, it's because you didn't have the balls to do what needed to be done!" he shouts over me.

That's it. That's what does it. We've been building to this for a long time, and now there's nothing to keep me from charging across the room, taking him by his collar, and hauling him in close. "You're fucking dead!"

"Try it!" he bellows, his spit flying in my face before he shoves me away with surprising strength. I stumble back and fall against a chair, tipping it onto its side and grabbing hold of Dante's shirt with my left hand, swinging at his jaw with my right. The moment of contact is sheer exhilaration. *Finally.* He's had it coming to him for too long.

The door to the study opens at the sound of our fighting, and in comes Vinny. "Get them off each other!" Papa bellows, and Vinny responds by placing his very sizable body between ours.

"You worthless son of a bitch." I snarl around Vinny's arm, swinging for Dante because, dammit, I need to hit somebody. I need to make somebody bleed. He's been begging for it for too long. Dante only rubs his reddened jaw, sneering.

"Stop. Right now, both of you." Papa stands, rounding his desk, and takes me by the back of the neck. "Enough of this. You aren't helping anyone by losing your grip on yourself. As for you..." he continues, taking hold of Dante with his other hand while Vinny backs off. "Like it or not, Emilia is part of the family now. It doesn't matter if you like it. That's the decision your brother made, and because we're family, we're going to respect that. If you can't accept it, it could be we have bigger problems than we thought."

"You know this is wrong," Dante insists. I can't remember the last time I saw him looking so intense, shaking, and practically spitting out every word. "This is only leading us deeper into war. Let's say we waste money and resources on finding her. What happens if we don't have what we need when they bring the fight to our doorstep? How do we protect Mama and Guilia and ourselves if that happens?"

"Don't pretend you care so much about them now," I growl out, which earns me a vicious squeeze from Papa. It could be he's not as weak as I thought, or the situation has him feeling as energized as I do. Ready to snap bones and crush skulls. I only need the opportunity.

"You aren't helping things," he snaps, scowling at me. "Your brother does make a good point. These are the factors we have to weigh. As much as we would like to pretend nothing else matters but what we want here and now, that isn't the way life works. Better you figure that out now than someday down the line when you have children of your own to protect."

"Fine..." I grunt for the sake of ending this and getting back to what matters. "I understand what you're saying."

"That won't change anything, will it?" Dante asks, scoffing.

Papa groans, releasing us. "I'm talking to myself." Shaking his head, he perches on the edge of his desk, blowing out a sigh.

I spare Dante one more dirty look before checking the time on my phone. Nine-thirty. How much damage could he do to her in such a short time? I shouldn't entertain the question. A world of pain could be inflicted in ninety minutes. "How the fuck did he know we were there?" My voice echoes throughout the room, but neither man can offer a response.

Turning on Dante, I snarl. "For all I know, you fucking tipped him off to get Emilia out of the way."

For once, he's caught off-guard. He quickly wipes away his wide-eyed shock. "You're out of your fucking mind," he scoffs. "We don't have time to go into all the reasons I would never do that."

"Luca..." Papa sighs. "Your brother would never do that to you."

"After what he said?" I counter. "Telling me this is how it was always going to be, and I should've put her out of her misery before this? Do you think he would stop at anything if he thought it would protect the family?"

My father holds up both hands, closing his eyes in silent surrender. "Stop wasting time and consider that this could be part of a larger play. It could be a means of flushing us out, weakening us before he launches a direct attack. We need to consider all possibilities before making a move."

"I understand." When Dante scoffs, I bear my teeth at him. "I mean it. I understand. So, if necessary, I'll take care of this by myself."

"How would you do that?" Dante asks, throwing his hands into the air. "This isn't Rambo. You're not going to go on a one-man killing spree."

"I'll do whatever it takes."

Papa rolls his eyes. "You're not going to do that. I'm not leaving you alone."

"You're seriously considering going after her?" Dante folds his arms, and I don't think we have ever had the balls to look at our father the way he is now. Like he's wondering about his sanity. "Papa. You know this is wrong."

"She's family now, which means *we* get her back," Papa decides. The tightness in my chest lessens slightly. I wasn't sure until now whether I had him on my side. It's one thing to feel sorry for me and be concerned for Emilia, but putting effort into bringing her home is another.

Dante backs away from us, hands in the air. "I'm through. Clearly, I'm the only person around here who gives a shit about what actually matters. Figure this out for yourselves. I'm going to bed since something tells me I'll need to be up bright and early to handle family business while you're distracted." With one last look of utter disgust, Dante marches from the room, slamming the door hard enough to shake the walls.

"He'll come around," Papa assures me, but I don't care. My brother is the least of my concerns now.

"I'm going to make some calls," Papa decides. "I'll get Craig on this, as well. You'll have him out there watching for her. We'll find her."

"I need to do something," I plead. I'm going to explode before much longer. We've wasted enough time already. Every passing second marks a second she could be in pain, scared, and needing me.

My father eyes me, his brows knitting together. "Why don't you go to the kitchen, get yourself something to eat, and have some coffee. You're going to need your strength. She's going to need you to be strong."

No. Not now. Not when she's suffering. I drop into the nearest chair, prepared to sit up all night if it comes to that.

He sighs and shakes his head like a worried father, placing his first call. "Rocco Santoro," he barks into the phone. "We need all eyes on Vitali's crew. He's picked up something belonging to us, and we're looking to get it back."

19

EMILIA

Until now, I've never known the meaning of humiliation. I keep my gaze lowered to the floor, focused on keeping my balance as I empty my bladder into a bucket. Someone's watching, I'm sure. This is probably the most entertainment they'll receive. Disgusting pigs.

I won't break down. I can stand a lot worse than this, even if I'm wracked with hunger, and my feet are practically numb from the cold. They haven't given me a blanket, nothing to keep warm. My teeth chatter before I can stop it, and I make it a point to tighten my jaw to maintain my composure.

It's clearly morning now, and what little I can see of the outside world tells me it's a gray, dreary day. Maybe it'll snow. It feels cold enough for it, but then I'm practically naked, locked in this dirty, grimy room.

I can't figure out what it was used for. Maybe it's a cell, and that's it. Maybe there are other people down here, locked away in their own prisons. I wonder if they're given water and food.

I haven't gotten any of either.

Luca has to be going crazy. I need to stay strong for him. They're trying to torture me into... what? Turning on the family? Granted, nobody has been in here to see me since that first visit when I regained consciousness, but I can only imagine that's the endgame. Either that, or I'm a pawn. It could be as simple as that, a means of hurting Luca and the rest of the family by holding me as bait.

In other words, I'm a liability when all I wanted was to be accepted by the Santoros. The idea makes me curl up tighter than ever on the bed, drawing my knees close to my chest and wrapping my arms around them.

I've never been cold like this. My head still aches, too, though at least the blood stopped flowing. There's a stain on the mattress thanks to the cut to my scalp, but there were already so many stains. Mine is just one more of them.

How can they find me here? Will they even know where to begin? I close my eyes and shudder, gritting my teeth in a desperate fight to hold myself together. So cold. So hungry.

To think, only yesterday, I was in that cozy café, with its little fireplace along the back wall and pleasant conversation all around us, eating that delicious breakfast, gazing at the man I love. It's amazing how life can turn on a dime. What I wouldn't give for some of that French toast now.

I'm on my way to what will be a beautiful dream about that meal and the happiness I felt yesterday when the lock clicks. My eyes snap open, and my breath catches. I don't know whether to be afraid of what comes next or be irritated at being interrupted. I was about to escape, at least in my head.

The door opens slowly, but I don't move. I'd rather find out first who I'm dealing with. Immediately, I catch a faint whiff of cologne. It almost reminds me of Luca's—musky, spicy—a far cry from the cheap shit my kidnappers wore. Right now, I would still take that over the lingering odor of piss that's filled the air ever since I first had to relieve myself last night.

My visitor clicks their tongue, standing at my back. "Such a shame. I'll bet he would have loved seeing you in this." Another tongue click.

"He's going to see me in it," I murmur, still facing the wall. Every cell in my body is keenly attuned to him, his presence, his deep voice, and the mock mourning in it. That's all any of this is. A mockery.

"Will he? Well, you might be right," he allows. "The question is, will you still be alive when he does? That's up to you, Detective Washington."

I don't have time to register surprise when he corrects himself. "Oh, forgive me. I forgot. You resigned, didn't you?" He's around half a second from laughing, the smug prick.

I have a pretty fair idea of who I'm talking to as I roll over and sit up to face him. Despite the ball cap shading his eyes, he's instantly recognizable. I've studied his picture the same way I knew I was looking at Luca the first time I laid eyes on him at the club. He has the same devilish good looks as Luca, though his features are thinner, almost delicate. His mother was a model before she met his father—a man many years her senior whose family is now under the control of his oldest son.

"Alessandro Vitali," I murmur, nodding my head. "I was wondering if we would ever get the chance to meet face to face."

His sensual lips stretch into a smile. "And here we are." He's dressed in sweats, and he must notice I'm studying him because he looks down at himself and snorts. "Swinging through on my way back from the gym. Forgive me for not looking my best."

He removes his black cap to reveal a head full of curly, chocolate-brown hair. He would be handsome if not for the hard, sharp glint in his eyes—hazel eyes that seem devoid of feeling as he glances around the room. "Not exactly the Plaza, is it?" he murmurs.

"It'll do." What, does he expect me to weep and whine? For fuck's sake. "What do you want with me?" I demand, still careful to keep any emotion out of my voice.

Another smile, but wider this time. "You are interesting. I can see why he likes you so much. I mean, right off the bat, you're... appealing." His gaze lingers on my chest when he says it, and I want to crawl into a hole and never come out.

Of course, he wants me to feel that, so I lift my chin and stare into his face like I don't notice. "Though I've gotta be honest with you," he continues with a sigh. "I don't go for mouthy bitches."

"And I'm sure every mouthy bitch in North America just sighed in disappointment," I murmur with a faint smile.

He blurts out the sort of laugh that means genuine surprise. "Hell, I might decide to keep you for myself," he muses, folding his arms over what is clearly a thick chest beneath his hoodie. He takes care of himself, so much so he could snap my neck like a twig. "I mean, I had no idea you'd be so interesting."

"I have my moments." What is he getting at? What does this mean?

"So if I were to ask you what you know about the Santoro family and their business, you would entertain me with all sorts of stories. Right?" he prompts, still grinning like we're old friends.

"No," I respond flatly. "I wouldn't."

"So you say now." He rocks back on his heels, smirking. "We'll see how you feel in another day or so. When you're so cold, you can't feel your body. So hungry and thirsty, you would agree to anything so long as you get a sip of water."

"Keep telling yourself that if it makes you feel better," I snap, and his eyes flash, telling me I've gone too far, but I'm not about to back down now. "I have nothing to tell you," I insist as firmly as possible. I show no fear, panic, and begging. It's the truth, after all. "You think they would tell me anything? They still don't trust me. Most of them resent me being around. I'm not just a woman. I'm an ex-cop."

"You're full of shit." He snarls, and this is the real Alessandro. The mask has fallen, and he doesn't bother putting it back into place. His formerly handsome face twists into something vicious, cruel, and full of hatred. "You've got Luca so twisted up, he would do anything. He'd say anything. He probably rattles off critical information while you're sucking his little pencil dick. Don't give me that bullshit story."

"It's the truth," I tell him with a defeated sigh. "Really. I don't know anything more than you do. Hell, you probably know more than me. I mean it. You're wasting your time." I even shrug as I stare up at him.

"We'll see about that." He purses his lips to emit a high-pitched whistle. His two thugs practically trot into the room like the trained dogs they are. The one with the black eye looks even worse than last night, and the one whose face I slashed is using butterfly stitches to keep the wound closed.

Alessandro draws a deep breath, then looks down at the floor, backing away from the bed. "Do it," he mutters.

I have no time to process his words before the man with the black eye shoves me onto the bed and pins me, holding me down so hard my already sore muscles scream in protest.

"What? Stop!" I grunt, kicking and squirming. "What are you—"

A fist comes at me, and my instincts kick in. I try to dodge, but it's too late. The blow connects with brutal force, driving all the air out of my lungs. I roll over, clutching my stomach, struggling to breathe.

That's when I see the side of a knife held by the man I slashed silences me. It makes me go still as I try not to pass out from the pain while my entire field of vision narrows to the blade, gleaming faintly in the gray morning light. "You just relax now," he urges with a bitter, humorless laugh.

My heart is pounding out of my chest, and there's still a scream locked behind my clenched teeth, but I'm afraid to make a sound or move. All I can do is stare in growing terror at the knife as it comes closer and closer, tormenting me.

"Get it over with," Alessandro orders from behind him, sounding bored.

I cringe, sucking in a terrified gasp as a handful of my hair is taken, then pulled straight up and away from my head. The knife comes closer, and I let out a silent scream before it begins to slice through my hair, the motions savage and painful.

Hot, furious tears of shame and sorrow roll down the sides of my face. I'm barely able to bite back the sobs wracking my body as one handful after another is brutally cut away from my head. The men, Alessandro included, joke among themselves about how much Luca is going to like his present.

Finally, Alessandro clears his throat. "One last parting gift," he says, giving his solider a nod. Before I can comprehend what's happening, a sharp burning sensation rips through me. I let out a throaty gasp as my gaze sinks to where the knife's tip has slashed across my hand, and blood begins to trickle down my arm.

From the corner of my eye, I see someone taking a photograph of me, and I know why.

"That will do." As quickly as it began, it's over, both men backing away and gathering up most of the hair spread out around my head while I'm left applying pressure to the stinging sharp cut that is so fucking painful I can barely breathe.

"We'll give you some time to search your memory," Alessandro offers, standing by the door while I raise a shaking hand to my head. "Maybe you'll be a little more forthcoming once it's time for us to have a conversation about how you can help my family. If you know what's good for you," he adds, the words heavy with meaning.

He leaves before I can say a word, not that there's anything to be said. I can only run my hand over my head, where my hair sits in clumpy patches of all different lengths. I'm glad I can't see the disaster they've turned me into. I don't think I could handle it. I can barely stand touching it, especially when I reach a spot where the hair is chopped nearly down to my scalp.

That's what does it. That's the straw that breaks the camel's back. This time, when I curl up facing the wall, there's no way to keep the tears from flowing.

20

LUCA

I didn't mean to fall asleep.

My plan was to stay awake, waiting, going from one heartbeat to the next. Barely breathing, able to think about nothing but Emilia. What she's going through, whether she believes I'll find her, whether she is losing hope. If she's hurt, bleeding, maybe dying...

How can I sleep at a time like this? No matter how Mama pestered me or Guilia tearfully urged me to get something to eat, I'm not interested. I wasn't exactly gentle when I told them so.

Yet sleep caught up to me anyway. By the time I rise with a start, the ornate clock on my father's desk tells me I was out for two hours. What might've happened since then? What if I missed something?

The pounding of feet in the hall and raised voices are what woke me. I run to the door and throw it open not a moment before Dante shoves his way into the room. He's holding the corner of a manilla envelope between two fingers. "This came in just now. They're reviewing the security footage down at the guard house, hoping to get a look at the plates." He's out of breath like he's been running.

"Someone left it here?" I ask, wondering what it means and what it has to do with Emilia.

"Threw it from a passing van." He thrusts it my way, and now I see my name scrawled in block letters across the front, etched in black marker.

"We should wait for Papa," Dante urges, but I'm already bending the metal prongs holding the envelope shot. His hand wraps around my wrist in a death grip, stopping me. "It might not be safe."

Considering the envelope weighs nothing, I can't imagine anything inside could harm us. A box would be a different story. I might hesitate to open it.

"There's nothing dangerous inside," I insist, freeing my wrist. "Feel free to run away if you're scared." He scowls but doesn't move.

Flipping back the flap, I ease the envelope open and peer inside. At first, I don't know what I'm looking at. "What is it?" Dante demands.

I shake my head, going to the window to get a better look. It can't be what it looks like. I'm seeing things. Yet when I hold the envelope open in the light, it's obvious.

"Oh my God. Oh God." That's all I can say, the only words my mouth will form as I stare blankly into the envelope and study its contents.

"What is it?" Dante tries to tear the envelope from my hands, but I only tighten my grip, squeezing it in my fist when blank rage sweeps over me. Something falls out and drifts to the floor, and he picks it up, studying it.

"Hair?" he asks, almost laughing at the absurdity. "They sent you hair?"

"It's hers. It's *her* hair," I choke out, looking inside again.

Something is sitting at the bottom of the envelope. I pull out the folded paper when I do, a small photograph falls out.

I feel Dante beside me when I turn it over.

I can barely make it out, but it's her. Pale, roughed up, with her hand covered in blood. Oh God, I feel physically ill. What have they fucking done to my beautiful angel?

My eyes reluctantly peel away from her photograph to the note.

Imagine what I'll cut off next time.

Guilt folds me in half, leaving me bent over and gasping for air before my knees give out. I fall to them because now it's real. Now, I'm holding the evidence in my hands. He's hurt her. He's made a mockery of her, all for the sake of breaking me.

At the moment, it feels like he has. "Luca," Dante murmurs, reminding me he's in the room.

"I was going to propose." Reaching into the envelope, I take a handful of the silky locks I ran my hands through while she slept in my arms in front of the fire only yesterday when everything was different. When all I knew was hope.

"What?" He comes closer, touching a hand on my shoulder. "What are you saying?"

"Last night. I was going to ask her to marry me." I hold the hair to my cheek and close my eyes. It still smells like her. Wasn't I going to buy her a lifetime supply of whatever they used on it at the salon? I'm losing it, finally.

"Fuck." His grip tightens slightly before he lets go. "I didn't know that."

"There's a lot you don't know," I mutter, choking back tears. When was the last time I cried? No idea. Maybe when I broke my arm when I was a kid.

My best friend betrayed me, and I beat him to death for it, but I never shed a tear.

This is Emilia. They hurt what's mine. They're fucking with her head to fuck with me. Shaming her, humiliating her by cutting off her hair, and probably mocking her while they did. Damn right, I feel something.

Looking up at my brother, I see something I didn't know I needed—understanding, even sympathy. It's like he gets it, and this is what it took to make him understand.

This was never a game for me. I wasn't fucking around with some random nobody for the sake of getting my dick wet. I wasn't sacrificing my family over a woman who meant nothing.

"They're going to kill her," I choke out. Saying the words is enough to make bile rush into my throat, but I swallow it back. She needs me to be strong, dammit.

"We'll find her before that happens." He's certain of it, wearing a determined expression I've seen countless times. Normally, he wears it while he's glaring at me, giving me shit for something or other.

When he extends a hand, I take it, and he helps me off my knees. As I watch, he sits at Papa's desk and picks up the phone. "He's upstairs resting," he explains, cutting off my chance to ask. "Mama wouldn't take no for an answer."

"Who are you calling?" I ask.

"The guard house." He holds up a finger. "What do you have down there?"

I watch as he scribbles a letter and four numbers on a notepad. They got partial plates. Craig could run it along with a description of the van. He might be able to track down traffic cam footage. Something, anything to track the van's progress. If the hair came from Emilia, chances are good that the guy who delivered the envelope came from the location where she's being held.

Reading my mind, Dante ends the call but starts a new one. "Craig's burner," he explains.

"Let me talk to him." I curl my fingers in a beckoning gesture, and he hands me the receiver without arguing, sitting back and letting me take the lead.

"Hello?" Craig's voice is tight, maybe even full of suspicion when he answers.

There's no time for pleasantries, not that I would bother when it comes to him. We might need him, but that doesn't mean I have much respect for him. "Are you free to offer an update?" I ask. He could be in mixed company and unable to speak freely.

"Yes, certainly." There's a business-like tone in his voice now, like he's chatting with a repairman or something. "There has been increased activity in certain circles."

My heart was already pounding, but now it's racing. "Any indication of a location?" I ask.

"Not yet, but we're searching." He lowers his voice until it's close to a whisper. "They've been talking about a guest. Last night, word started to spread. No specifics yet."

"Just got a package here," I inform him, looking down at Dante's notes. "Security footage gives us partial plates and a description of the vehicle."

After taking down the information, Craig asks, "What sort of package?"

My throat closes to a pinhole. I should refuse to answer. It's none of his concern. Yet he knows her. It might light a fire under his ass and make him work harder. "He sent me her hair."

"Fuck," Craig groans out after a moment's silence. "That sick bastard."

"He won't be satisfied stopping at that for long," I grit out. There's no shaking the mental image of my Emilia shaking, weeping, begging them to stop. No, she wouldn't beg.

"You don't have to tell me that." He clears his throat before his voice returns to its former volume. "We're searching known hideouts, properties the family owns. It's an extensive list, though, and I can't dedicate too much manpower to it without a concrete reason. Unless you want me to get into specifics."

"No. We want to keep this quiet." That much isn't going to change. No spreading the word around. No letting this get out to law enforcement beyond our hand-picked few.

"You know I'm doing everything I can. And not just for you," he adds, sounding gruff.

"I don't care who you're doing it for. Just get it done. Find out where they took her. We'll handle the rest." I hang up the receiver, not interested in his response.

We have a lead. We're that much closer. "We're going to get her back," I tell my brother, who nods firmly.

We've finally found something we can agree on. I know better than to think it'll last long, but it's good enough for now.

21

EMILIA

It's been dark for hours or what feels like it.

I watched the light from the window travel across the wall as the day progressed until finally, the light was gone, and night fell. The worst part is not knowing how much time has passed. I don't have the faintest idea how late it is. It could be tomorrow morning, for all I know.

I'm so thirsty. All I can think about is having something to drink. Even the gnawing hunger and the worsening cold aren't as intense as my thirst.

There have been voices outside the door, though that was probably meant as a way to scare me. Nobody has come in since Alessandro visited this morning. It was much more fun for them to stand outside and talk about all of the things they wanted to do to me. They wanted to hurt me, to cut the dress away from my body, to spread me open wide and...

I force myself to shake my head and squeeze those ugly thoughts away. That's how they win. They get into my head and make me imagine the things they describe. I'm stronger than this. I'm not going to fall for their trap.

At least, that's what I tell myself. Every hour that passes

leaves me a little less certain of my strength because every hour that passes leaves these guys feeling bolder. Like they're going to get away with it. And there's no telling what a man will do when he's got an idea in his head.

Luca, you need to hurry.

I should get up. I should force myself to get some exercise to get my blood pumping. The idea of stretching out is too much to stand, though. As cold as I am all curled into a ball, it's so much worse when I'm not huddled up. There has to be a limit to how long I can stand this, right? I'm not cold enough to freeze to death—at least, I don't think so—but who's to say? Eventually, my body is going to break down. With no food or water, and my teeth chattering miserably, I can't endure it forever. No one could.

The worst part is, I've probably been here around twenty-four hours. Maybe thirty. Hardly more than a day, but it seems like an eternity of misery has passed.

The part that makes me tremble with revulsion is how my heart leaps not with fear but with hope when the lock on my door clicks loudly. Hope that they're bringing me water, a blanket, and food. I force myself to sit up, my stiff muscles awkward and slow to obey. Somehow, there's still part of me that won't allow me to show weakness, at least not while they're in the room with me.

I groan inwardly at the sight of the men who kidnapped me, along with another two men I don't recognize. What are they doing that they need four men? Fear uncoils in my belly like a snake. They're not here to sit down and have a chat.

"Not so feisty now, are you?" the man with the black eye snickers, elbowing his friend. "Not so pretty anymore, either."

"I would say the same to you, only you weren't pretty in

the first place," I retort, and one of the men behind them snickers, trying to cover it up with a cough.

All he does is offer a cold smile full of nastiness. "I'm going to fucking love this." He sighs, like a man who's been looking forward to a big event that's finally arrived.

Then they're on me, taking me by the arms, hauling me to my feet. Panic explodes in my head, and instinct leaves me fighting, kicking, and snarling at them. "Get your fucking hands off me!" It's amazing how loud I can scream when I'm so weak.

"That's right." One of the men laughs as they drag me from the room and into the brightly lit hallway. "Keep fighting. Like it'll do you any good."

Even the stale air in the hallway outside the room is better than the stench of piss. Fluorescent lighting casts a bluish glare that leaves me blinking hard after hours spent in near darkness. My head swings around as I try desperately to get a sense of where I am or where I'd have to run to escape. I don't see an exit, though, only more doors leading to more rooms. Where the hell are we?

We turn a corner, and I realize they're leading me to an open door. In an instant, I notice what's spread out on the floor inside. "What is this? What are you doing? Get off me! You bastards!" My bare feet slide across the floor no matter how I try to plant them, to make myself immovable. It's no use. They drag me into the room with plastic sheets spread out beneath a single wooden chair.

It's like Luca's office, the night we met. There's plastic everywhere. They're going to make me bleed. A fresh burst of adrenaline makes me kick and scream, and my foot connects with the chair and knocks it over before one of the guards backhands me hard enough to make my head snap to the side. "Stop wasting your fucking time," he snarls out while I bite back a cry of pain and taste blood in my mouth. Soon, the chair is upright, and I'm slammed into it, my hands zip-tied behind me, and my ankles zip-tied to the legs.

"All this fighting and struggling." His voice rings out over the rushing of blood in my ears just as he comes in, smooth, silky, and deceptively gentle. I force myself to look up into Alessandro's cold eyes, as defiant as possible while quaking and screaming inside.

This is it. This is where I die, where my story ends, and Luca never came. In my heart, I know he tried, but there wasn't enough time. I only hope he'll believe I did my best for him. That I never broke down. It stiffens my spine and helps me sit upright to glare at my captor without trembling.

I won't be a coward.

"Look at you." Alessandro shakes his head mournfully, his dark curls gleaming in the light from the overhead bulb. This room is just like the one I came from, except there's no bed. A storage facility, maybe? It could be. I'll never know for sure, will I?

"That's going to bruise," he murmurs, brushing the backs of his fingers over his cheek, indicating the place where my face throbs after I was slapped.

"I think I can handle it," I mutter, pretending the ache doesn't have me fighting back tears.

"I bet you can." His smile seems almost genuine. "For what it's worth, I wish I had found you first. I would like to get to know you better," he murmurs softly like he approves.

"Am I supposed to be flattered?" I ask, scoffing. "Because I'm not. Your opinion doesn't mean shit."

"Hey, nobody can say I didn't try to be friendly." He folds his arms, stepping back and glancing at the men standing behind me. With a slight nod, one of them steps up beside me, and I catch the way his fists clench and release from the corner of my eye. He's getting himself ready.

Alessandro levels a hard gaze my way, lowering his brow. No more Mr. Nice Guy. "Tell me everything you know about the Santoro family. What they're planning. Where they intend to attack what's mine."

"I already told you," I report in a flat voice. "I have nothing to offer."

His snarl is ugly, promising pain. "And I'm telling you, you're full of shit. Men talk. When they're in bed with their woman, they share things."

"That might be true for you, but that's not how Luca does it." I can't help but grin. "We're usually doing other things in bed besides talking."

He snorts. "So what you're telling me is, you were just a hole for him to fill."

"Is that supposed to hurt my feelings?" I ask with a laugh.

His steely gaze darts to the man next to me. Like magic, pain explodes across my face, starting at the place where the guard's fist makes contact. I've never been hit like this. There's a moment when everything goes numb like my brain doesn't know how to process the sensation before there's nothing left but agony. I open and close my mouth a few times to make sure my jaw is still intact, then spit out a mouth full of blood.

"Let's try again," Alessandro murmurs as smoothly as ever. "How much of my territory do they plan on taking? Where are they going to start? Gambling? Maybe tipping off the DEA and having my trade halted? Who do they have on the inside?"

"You are wasting your time," I insist. "I don't know anything."

Again, fresh pain blooms, hot and furious, this time on the other side of my face. I feel the place where the skin over my cheekbone has split, where blood now trickles over my skin and drips onto my chest while I hang my head. A sudden, sharp blow to my stomach makes my head fall back and knocks the air from my lungs. I gasp and strain to pull breath into my body. I finally do, though right now, I'm not sure if I wouldn't rather pass out. At least I wouldn't feel anything.

"This isn't going to stop until you give me what I want," Alessandro informs me, cool and matter-of-fact.

I slowly, carefully draw a breath, wincing when my bruised muscles protest. Raising my head again, I glare at him, whispering, "Go to hell and take these assholes with you."

"Maybe we need to stuff her mouth full of cock," one of the guys mutters, grasping my jaw, leaving me gritting my teeth to hold back a scream of pain as my already bruised, throbbing flesh aches worse than ever.

"We aren't animals," Alessandro murmurs, scornful. "We won't be doing that tonight. And she can't give me what I need with her mouth full, anyway."

The man shoves my face away, and I gasp for air, furious with myself, when a single tear rolls down my cheek. "He's going to kill you for this," I whisper, and the thought stirs a bitter laugh in my throat. "He'll make you watch him carve parts of you away before he finally digs the eyes out of your skull."

Alessandro takes one slow step toward me, then another. "The way he murdered his best friend? Right there in the office of his shitty club? You ought to know. You were there," he reminds me in an almost playful voice, a cat toying with a wounded mouse before discarding it.

A sick chill runs through me. It's not like I didn't already flash back to that night earlier, but somehow it's worse to hear him talk about it. "You don't know what you're talking about," I whisper.

"No? And I guess I don't know about the bullshit story the family concocted to cover up your disappearance?" he counters lightly. "How they bickered over whether you would live or die? How you offered to resign to stay alive?" Only those hard, glittering eyes give away the coldness inside him.

Somehow, in the middle of the pain consuming my every thought, the truth trickles in. "How do you know about that?" I whisper.

Soft, knowing laughter rings out around me when Alessandro replies, "What? You thought your former partner was only working for the Santoros?" After taking a moment to watch sickening understanding settle over me, he glances toward the men.

Then he nods.

The real pain begins.

22

LUCA

"I told you, I've had enough." I might as well be speaking to the wall. My mother insists on heaping more pasta into my bowl no matter what I say. I've barely touched what was in there, forcing a few swallows worth of the spicy rigatoni and sausage, though I hardly tasted it.

The sun has set again, and there's still nothing about Vitali's so-called guest. Nothing about the van. We haven't heard another word from him, either. No more deliveries. No phone calls.

What the fuck is he waiting for? I push the bowl away from me rather than throw it across the room. It would only scare Mama, and she doesn't deserve it. She's been puttering around the house all day, and twice, I've caught her weeping softly when she didn't think anyone was around. She's only trying to do what she can. Even now, I see that.

This isn't the first crisis she's been through. Beneath her softness and sweetness, a steel core is at the center. That's the only reason she and my father managed to have such a successful marriage, so full of love. I didn't get my resilience from Papa alone.

When Dante and Cesco join us, she pulls two bowls from the cabinet. "There's food here on the stove, keeping warm," she tells them, then wipes down the counter for the third time since I allowed her to bully me into sitting in the kitchen.

She cleans when she's anxious, but only once she's finished cooking.

"You know I love your spicy rigatoni," Cesco tells her. He's always had a soft spot for her, probably the only one he possesses. I want to ask why he's here and not out hunting for Emilia, cutting down anyone who gets in the way, but there are already men out on the streets searching for Alessandro or any of his closest friends. As far as we can tell, they're ghosts, blown away in the fucking wind.

Dante eats, standing by the counter, shoveling the food in like a machine, completing a task before it can move on to the next. "Thank you, Mama," he murmurs when he's finished, giving her a brief smile as he places the bowl in the sink.

His phone buzzes, and he reaches into his pocket, his eyes widening once he checks the screen. "Craig." He meets my gaze from across the room, raising the phone to his ear. "Craig? What do you have?"

I rise, my heart in my throat, while Cesco waits with the fork halfway to his mouth. He only lowers it when Dante nods firmly. "I know the area. Thank you," Dante adds. "We won't forget this."

"What does he have?" I demand, aware of how Mama jumps when my sharp question echoes in the room.

"A location. The van was spotted leaving a storage facility on the edge of Queens." He's already on his way across the kitchen with Cesco behind him. "It belongs to a holding company registered to the Vitali family."

I break into a run, and even over my frantic heartbeat, I hear my brother and cousin behind me. Dante calls for Nico when we cross paths near the front door, then shouts for two of our guards to join us once we're outside, where a row of SUVs awaits. Let him figure out the logistics. It's what he does best. All I care about is getting to her fast.

"I'll drive!" Nico announces, and as much as I would rather be the one behind the wheel, it's probably safer for him to do it when I'm like this. I'm consumed by rage, and the question of whether we're already too late is on repeat.

I throw myself into the passenger seat, and Dante climbs in behind me while Cesco and the others take a second vehicle. Dante shouts the address through his open window so Cesco will know where to go before Nico pulls away, sending gravel flying as we tear down the driveway.

"There's a chance she's not there," Dante reminds me, but his voice is only one of so many others screaming inside my skull. Voices blaming me, cursing me, begging me. They all sound like Emilia, her sweet, husky voice, one that called my name in ecstasy and whispered it tearfully. She has to be alive. She has to be well. We have to get through this. What do I do otherwise? What is there to live for?

But how would I live knowing I couldn't protect her?

"We're about twenty minutes away," Nico informs us after plugging the address into his GPS with one hand while steering with the other. "I can make it fifteen."

"Then do it," I grit out, checking my pistol, pulling a second from the glove box, and making sure it's ready.

"If she's there, she'll be heavily guarded," Dante tells me as if I need to be told. I don't have it in me to inform him I've already been through every possibility. I've played it out countless times over these agonizing hours.

The world around us flashes past in a blur thanks to Nico's fearless driving. Every minute takes us closer, heightening the painful questions reverberating in my head like a gong. What if we're too late? What if what they did can't be undone? What if she's still alive and hates me for letting this happen? That might be the worst outcome. Not only hating myself but knowing she hates me.

The area goes from residential to industrial, and soon, we're approaching a cluster of office parks, gray, bland, and practically identical. Beyond that, the beginnings of yet another storage facility sit behind a chain-link fence. A handful of long cinderblock boxes look completed while a half-dozen are in progress. Did they dump her here somewhere?

"This is it," Dante grunts out. "This is where the van came from."

Nico slows down and cuts the headlights. In the passenger side mirror, I see Cesco doing the same thing. After racing here, I could scream at the infuriating crawl we've slowed too, even if I understand why. We could be wasting precious time.

"Up ahead," Nico points out as we take a tour of the area, rolling slowly past one structure after another. A dark blue truck, the only vehicle we've seen since arriving, is parked in front of one of them. I hold up a hand, and Nico hits the brakes, putting the SUV in park a few dozen yards away from the truck. Cesco does the same, and moments later, we're exiting the vehicles, guns drawn, staying close to the wall leading to a metal door that's been propped open with a brick. There's a light burning inside, but otherwise, there's no sign of life. *Please, be inside. Please, be alive.* I will do anything, give anything, down to my own life so long as she survives.

I hear the shuffling footsteps a split second before the door swings open from the inside, followed by two men who burst out, firing wildly. Cesco expertly takes one of them out with no hesitation, the body hitting the ground with a bullet between the eyes. Nico takes the other, and the bastard falls against the open door, his body sliding down its length until it lands in a heap. Deafening silence follows. No more footsteps, no shouts from inside.

"Be careful!" Dante urges, but I barely hear him.

If only one truck was left behind, there can't be many men around. They might have been the only two. I hope they aren't since I would like to shed blood tonight too. But even that isn't as important as finding Emilia.

"I'll take the basement level," Dante offers, already halfway down the concrete stairwell to the right of the entrance. "You look up here."

Nico falls in step beside me, the two of us running down one seemingly endless hall after another and finding nothing but closed doors. The entire facility isn't finished being constructed yet, meaning the units aren't in use, so their doors are unlocked for us to fling them open one after another.

I hear it before Nico does, holding up a hand and freezing in silence, then I hear it again. Dante's voice. "Luca! Down here!" he shouts from the basement.

Taking off at a sprint, I trace my steps, taking the stairs. We collide at the bottom like he is running to find me. I steady myself, grabbing him by the shoulders. "Where?" I grunt out, ready to push him aside.

He tries to stop me, remaining in place when I try to get past him. "Luca, I don't think she—"

No, I'm not hearing this. I refuse. "Where is she?" I scream, noting his resigned sigh and refusing to accept it.

He grimaces but takes off running, leading me around the corner where a door sits open. I barely register the blood-stained plastic sheeting covering the floor as I take in the sight of the bruised, bloody mass curled up in the middle of it.

It's not moving. *She's* not moving.

"I couldn't get a pulse," Dante grunts as I drop to my knees. Rage and revulsion so intense it could paralyze me, fight for control while I slowly, gently roll her onto her back.

She's hardly recognizable, thanks to the blood that's covered most of her face. There's a cut along her cheekbone, a large abrasion covering most of her chin and half of her jaw. Her shorn hair is sticky, now a rusty red instead of its normal chestnut brown.

"Oh, baby, no." I lift her in my arms as gently as I can and hold her close to my chest. She's so cold. I have to warm her up. "Please, please, wake up. You have to wake up. Emilia, please." Her head lolls against my shoulder, her body still. Lifeless.

"Check again," Dante urges, kneeling beside me. "I might've missed it."

I hear him, but I feel her. How cold she is. How stiff. My anguished cry echoes in the tight space. "God, no," I moan out, rocking her, lost in grief and shock. She can't be dead. I can't lose everything.

Nico drops to one knee in front of me. "Set her down. Let go of her." When he makes the mistake of trying to pull her from my grasp, I clutch her closer, screaming my rage. He still won't let up, finally settling for pressing fingers to her neck.

With his other hand, he grips my shoulder. "I think I feel something. Set her down, goddammit!"

I don't. I can't let her go when she's this cold. But I do press an ear to her chest, ignoring the dried trails of blood that paint her skin. I close my eyes, holding my breath, waiting.

There it is—a faint heartbeat. It's not my imagination. "Get the car!" I bark out, and he takes off running along with my brother while I lift her, getting to my feet. As gently as I can, I run from the room. "Hold on, baby," I plead. "Hold on. Don't leave me."

Dante is waiting outside beside the open door to the rear of the SUV. "She needs a hospital!" I demand, and he helps me get her into the back seat before I follow, lifting her head and cradling it in my lap so I can gaze down at her bloody, swollen face.

"Drive!" I scream, though we're already moving. Not fast enough. Nothing short of flying would be fast enough.

Dante calls out orders to Nico, then barks into his phone. "We're coming in with a wounded woman," he tells whoever is on the other end of the call. "It looks like she's been badly beaten, and we can only find a faint pulse. We're going to need a room for her. No, not triage." He snarls. "We're taking her up to a private room. And you're going to have it ready when we arrive. Do you think I give a fuck?" he shouts while Nico takes a corner without slowing down, making horns blare while the tires squeal.

I reach out and take the phone from him, holding it to my ear. A woman is babbling some useless bullshit about procedures and protocol, but I cut her off. "This is Luca Santoro," I tell her, holding Emilia's head still with my other hand when Nico takes another sharp turn. "And I don't care what it takes. I will build your hospital a new wing if I have to in repayment, but you will take her straight up to a private room. No names will be used. Doctors and nurses will treat her discreetly. She's unconscious, barely breathing. It appears she has a head wound." Her blood is seeping into my pants as I speak. Her heart is still pumping, if weakly.

"Sir, she will need to be assessed in triage," the woman insists.

"Fuck triage!" I shout. "And fuck *you* if you don't do what I say. I will have your goddamn job, do you understand? We'll be there in..."

"Three minutes," Nico grunts as we blow through a red light.

"Three minutes," I repeat. "Be ready."

They're ready.

A pair of nurses stand outside the main entrance to the hospital with a gurney between them. Dante helps me get Emilia out of the car, and together, we lay her across the gurney, following the nurses who rush it inside. I don't know the answers to most of the questions they fire at us—whether she's allergic to any medications, her blood type, her medical history. There hasn't been time to learn those things. *We haven't had enough time.*

As for how she ended up this way, that's a question with a heavier weight. For once, I'm glad my brother exists since he takes charge. "She's a close friend of our family," he explains in the elevator. "We found her this way. That's as much as I can tell you, for your sake," he adds.

I glance up from Emilia's limp body in time to witness the nervous glance they exchange. "Help her," I whisper, holding her hand. "Do whatever it takes. I'll pay for all of it. Spare nothing."

When the doors open, the nurses rush in with the gurney. "You'll have to stay in the family waiting area outside her room," one of them barks out at me while the other hits a button on the wall, automatically opening a large pair of doors. This is clearly where the hospital's most affluent patients stay, in rooms split in half to allow their loved ones to set up camp comfortably.

The nurses take Emilia to the other half of the closest room, where a bed and equipment wait. When I try to follow them inside, Dante takes me by the arm. "Let them do their jobs," he urges in a tight voice.

"Get off me," I warn, growling and pulling away, but he's determined to drag me away from Emilia and into the waiting area on the other side of the glass doors, which are quickly closed behind us. There's nothing to do but watch helplessly from the next room as a nurse pulls the curtains, cutting me off from the center of my world.

Some generic talking head reads the news from a flatscreen television mounted against the wall behind me, droning on while I turn in a slow circle. The room is full of plush sofas and chairs. A full private bathroom and refrigerator are in the corner from which Dante pulls out a bottle of water. After gulping half of it down, he sighs. "They know what they're doing. She's going to pull through."

I need to believe that. It's the only thing holding me together as I drop into one of the chairs and hold my head in my hands. I hear voices overlapping in there, orders being barked back and forth.

What does she need? What's it going to take to make her well?

Hours pass. Dante only leaves when somebody from the house comes with clothes for me to change into. "You don't want her seeing you like this when she wakes up," he tells me, thrusting the bag into my lap when I can't be bothered to accept it.

Vinny arrives to keep watch. Dante keeps Papa updated over the phone when I can't bring myself to speak. Night turns to morning. Somebody brings food. I barely notice any of it. Why haven't they told me anything? Why hasn't she woken up?

It's past nine by the time a middle-aged man in scrubs enters the room, looking around. "Who is responsible for this girl?" he asks in a weary voice.

"She's my fiancée," I announce, springing from the chair and crossing the room in a few long strides. It doesn't matter that it's not technically true. "How is she? Has she woken up?"

He eyes me warily. "Somebody beat the hell out of her. Besides her face, there are bruised ribs, a lacerated liver and spleen, and ligature marks around the wrists and ankles," he announces, and it's clear he's decided I'm the culprit.

"You know who I am," I mutter, barely controlling myself after waiting hours to be accused. "Don't pretend you haven't heard my name since we got here. Suffice it to say my family has enemies. I'm going to leave it at that for your sake, not mine. Understand what I'm trying to explain?" I ask.

"I'm not intimidated by your name or the names of your enemies," he replies smoothly. "But this wouldn't be the first time a panicked man brought a woman in here—"

"Forget that shit. How is she?" Dante demands behind me.

The doctor only sighs. "She was in bad shape when you got here... dehydrated, low body temperature, but of course, the wound to the side of her head was the most critical. We performed a scan, which confirmed minor swelling to the brain, but she's improved greatly over the past several hours."

"Improved?" It's the only word I pick up on, the only one I understand. "Does that mean she's awake?"

Again, he sighs, and the concerned look he wears doesn't soften. "She is. But—"

Fuck anything else. She's awake. "I have to see her." I'm already pushing him aside, ignoring his protests, sliding open the glass door separating us and pulling back the curtain.

Relief steals my breath when I find Emilia lying in bed, raised partway with her bandaged head resting against the pillow. The stark reality of her wounds stands out now that the blood has been washed away. She's swollen, bruised, almost unrecognizable.

But she will heal.

What matters is she's alive, and she's mine. "Thank God," I groan out, rushing to her, almost throwing myself over her when I reach the bed. The relief is so intense, so raw. "You came back to me." I sob, clutching her, shaking. I got a second chance. This time, there will be no mistakes. I'm going to do everything right.

At first, I don't notice it. The way she squirms. The way she gasps. The way the slow, steady beeping of her heart monitor gets faster. "Wh-what?" She whimpers. "Who are you?" I lift my head, confused. She's terrified of me, her eyes wide, her breathing ragged and rapid. "What's happening?" she asks in a high-pitched whisper.

"Are you in shock?" I ask, searching her face for some sign of understanding. This is Emilia. My Emilia. Yet she shrinks away from me like we're strangers and shrieks when I try to touch her.

"Help!" she begs, finding the call button and jamming her thumb against it while I sputter in surprise.

The doctor reaches the bed and takes the button from

Emilia, patting her hand, careful of the IV taped in place. "Mr. Santoro," he murmurs, and now I see his sorrowful expression for what it is. "I wanted to explain before you saw her, but you didn't give me the chance."

"I don't understand." That's putting it mildly as I stand, stunned, while Emilia clutches a thin blanket against her chest and stares at me through bulging eyes. "What's wrong with her? You said she was improving. Is she still in shock?" I ask.

He shakes his head slowly. "It seems the injury to her brain has led to what we hope is temporary amnesia. As of now, she has no memory of who she is or what led to her being here."

There's nothing for me to do but watch in mute horror as a tear rolls down her cheek, staring at me like she's never seen me.

I've lost her.

To Be Continued...

WANT MORE?

Want read the final instalment between Luca and Emilia?

Finding Love is Book 3 in The Elite Mafia of New York out April 22nd.

Get it from Missy's Website or any good book retailer
https://authormissywalker.com/collections/elite-mafia-of-new-york-series

ALSO BY MISSY WALKER

*Forbidden Lust/Love are a duet and to be read in order.

*Cruel Lust is a trilogy and to be read in order

All other books are stand alones.

JOIN MISSY'S CLUB

Hear about exclusive book releases, teasers, discounts and book bundles before anyone else.

Sign up to Missy's newsletter here:
www.authormissywalker.com

Become part of Missy's Private Facebook Group where we chat all things books, releases and of course fun giveaways!

https://www.facebook.com/groups/missywalkersbookbabes

ACKNOWLEDGMENTS

Thanks to my editing team for their keen ears and sound advice.

To my betas, I adore reading your comments and suggestions to enhance my manuscript to the best of its potential. That's usually after I indulge in a block of chocolate upon realizing how much more work lies ahead to refine it!

Nevertheless, this business has toughened me up, and I wouldn't have it any other way.

To Mr. Walker, thank you for stepping in so much already this year. Being there more when I cannot. Marriage is a partnership, and I deeply appreciate everything you do for both the girls and me.

There is so much more I can't wait to share with you.

Missy x

ABOUT THE AUTHOR

Missy is an Australian author who writes kissing books with equal parts angst and steam. Stories about billionaires, forbidden romance, and second chances roll around in her mind probably more than they ought to.

When she's not writing, she's taking care of her two daughters and doting husband and conjuring up her next saucy plot.

Inspired by the acreage she lives on, Missy regularly distracts herself by visiting her orchard, baking naughty but delicious foods, and socialising with her girl squad.

Then there's her overweight cat—Charlie, chickens, and border collie dog—Benji if she needed another excuse to pass the time.

If you like Missy Walker's books, consider leaving a review and following her here:

instagram.com/missywalkerauthor
facebook.com/AuthorMissyWalker
tiktok.com/@authormissywalker
amazon.com.au/Missy-Walker
bookbub.com/profile/missy-walker

Printed in Great Britain
by Amazon